SPENS

Johnny

NOIR REUNION

Johnny Ostentatious

Active Bladder
PO Box 24607
Philadelphia, PA 19111
www.ActiveBladder.com

Noir Reunion © 2005 by John Osborn
Cover design: Kristina Moriconi
Proofreader: Lindsay Faith Rech (www.editingangel.tripod.com)

This is a work of fiction. Names, characters, places and incidents either are the product of the author's chemically-imbalanced imagination or are used fictitiously, and any resemblance to actual persons, living or dead, business establishments, events or locales is entirely coincidental. If you disagree, then you need to change the battery in your carbon-monoxide detector, 'cause you're higher than Stephen King during the writing of *Tommyknockers*.

Printed in the United States at:
Morris Publishing
3212 E. Hwy. 30
Kearney, NE 68847
800-650-7888
www.morrispublishing.com

All rights reserved. No part of this book may be reproduced or transmitted in any form or by any means, electronic, or mechanical, including photocopy, recording, or on any information storage and retrieval system, without permission in writing from the author or his cross-dressing parole officer, except by a punk-as-fuck reviewer who may quote brief passages in a critical article or review to be printed in a magazine or newspaper, or electronically transmitted on radio, television or the World Wide Web. Failure to do any or all of the above could result in the author performing a protest by refusing to shave his back for an entire week.

First printing: Fall 2005

ISBN 0-9761729-1-7

Dedicated to punk rock

2003

CHAPTER 1

Chase Kilbey was not what a casting director would call marketable. First off, he was thirty-seven years old—a relic in the eyes of Hollywood. Not to mention, he had a receding hairline that underscored his huge forehead. Plus, he had a mole on his left ear, which never failed to mesmerize the attention of passers-by. Despite all of this, his face radiated an inner strength that caused most people to warm to him instantly. Of course, his cobalt eyes might have had something to do with that.

Currently, Chase sat in his boss' office. His boss, Pierce Price, was on the phone, scolding a salesman.

"I don't care," Price bellowed into the mouthpiece. "We had a verbal agreement. When he buys six hundred units of *Oprah Experiencing an Orgasm*, then, and only then, does he get fifteen percent off the list price. Don't let him lowball you. You—What's that? No, you were going to say something. What was it? Say it. Go 'head. I'm listening. Uh-huh…uh-huh…yeah. You finished? Good. Now listen to me, don't turtle on this deal. Play hardball. I know this guy's type. If you give him an inch, he'll grab the whole freakin' yardstick. Be a man! Stick to your guns. If this asshole starts seriously backing out of the deal, simply lie and tell him we have a low profit margin on it. Say something like we're eating most of the shipping on this, so we can't budge on the price. If that doesn't work, try another tact. Use your imagination. Whatever you do, don't come back here until you sell those six hundred units for fifteen off list. If you come back with anything less, you're on the street."

Chase yawned. This was about as exciting as a 1990's John Hughes movie. The banter went on for a couple more minutes, Price ending each sentence with a finger jabbing the air, as if the caller could see him.

To pass time, Chase stared out the window. It was a sunny afternoon here in southern California. It was so sunny that even the P.M.-rush-hour smog couldn't block the bright rays. Chase leaned back. Sun glared off the office floor. He didn't mind. The glare blocked out a good portion of the industrial park's parking lot. The industrial park rented out space to a dozen businesses, one of which was Adult Entertainment Enterprises—Chase's employer.

Adult Entertainment Enterprises, or AEE as the stockholders called it, specialized in porn for every fetish there was a market for. Times were good for AEE. Thanks to the dot-com boom of the nineties, AEE reached millions of perverts that previously hadn't registered on the porn industry radar. The reason was elementary. Before the Internet, if you wanted adult-only material, you had to go to specialty stores deep inside the underbelly of American towns and cities—the kind of stores that neighbored between pool halls and cigar shops. But with the Internet, perverts could log online and effortlessly find anything their demented sex drives desired. And even though the dot-com gold rush ended years ago, AEE prospered more than *The Howard Stern Show*. AEE sold subscriptions and DVDs to its online customers and used most of that capital to strengthen its distribution to porn shops.

Chase closed his eyes. He couldn't believe he worked in such an immoral industry. Back in high school, if a fortuneteller had told him where he'd be today, he would've laughed in her face until his funny bone ached.

Chase opened his eyes and bowed his head. Strange how when you're young, you reach for the stars, but at middle age you discover you're still in the observatory.

Lifting his head, Chase stared out the window. The sun's glare was gone. He focused on the park across the street. A pair of eucalyptus trees waved back and forth in unison. Between the trees lay a wino. For a second, Chase envied him. That wino didn't have to get up early every morning and report to work for a ten-hour shift that paid slightly more than minimum wage. What Chase wouldn't give to leap out of his chair and storm out of his boss' office while giving him the finger. Chase smirked at that. How could he not? It was every workingman's fantasy. But he couldn't quit. He enjoyed crawling home each night to a warm bed and microwavable meal. And his wife, Monique, would kill him if he ever told his boss to *Sit and spin while I spit in your eye, you greedy motherfucker!* No way could Monique's job at the zoo cover their bills, even if Chase was unemployed for only a month. But all of that might be a moot point. If things worked out the way Chase hoped, he and Monique wouldn't have to worry about money for a long time. Maybe never.

Chase's boss slammed down the phone. Chase jumped imperceptibly. For a moment, he had forgotten where he was.

"Fucking sales rep," Price said. "He's calling me, asking for advice, right in front of the fucking client! Jesus, I knew I should've never hired anyone so green. So what can I do for you, Kilbey?"

"I just wanted to make sure—"

Price jumped out of his chair. The movement sent a whiff of his Drakkar cologne in Chase's direction. Chase tried not to gag.

Price stood in front of his fish tank. It ran the length of the wall behind his desk. He stepped to the left side of the tank and tapped the glass. The only fish in the tank, an oversized piranha, came to attention. It bared its teeth.

Price reached above the tank, the piranha's beady eyes following him. Price pulled down a fish bowl from an onyx shelf. Inside the bowl were four small koi, the largest one measuring only four inches long. They swam around in the bowl in a circle, none of them leading. *It's almost like a chain*, Chase thought.

Price's hand dove into the fish bowl. The koi ignored him. Price's hand swerved around in the bowl like a shark. Using his thumb and index finger, he pinched the tail fin of one of the hapless koi and yanked it out of the bowl. The other three koi quit swimming around in a circle. They stared up at the rim of the fish bowl, their mouths open in confusion, barbels dangling.

Price returned the fish bowl to the shelf. The koi hanging from his hand tried to flail free. Price pinched the tail fin harder. The koi's gills fluttered.

Johnny Ostentatious

With his free hand, Price opened a section of the fish tank lid. The piranha was unable to leap up and bite the hand that was about to feed it because of a perforated plastic compartment near the top of the tank. The compartment was six inches in diameter. The piranha gravitated towards it. Price dropped the koi into the compartment. Water splashed onto Price's gold bracelet. He closed the fish tank lid.

The koi surveyed its new quarters. The piranha attacked, its fangs digging into the compartment's holes, scratching the plastic. The entire tank shook. Sensing its fate, the koi pressed against the lid of the tank. Price, smiling, pressed a button on the lid. The compartment collapsed; the four sides snapped to the top of the lid, as did the bottom of the compartment due to a hinge that hooked to one of the sides. Predictably, the piranha lunged for the koi. The koi swam away and gave the piranha a good chase, but it was no use. This was the predator's home turf, and—more importantly—it was hungry. Chase knew the piranha was starving. His boss constantly bragged how he only fed it once a week.

Price, still smirking, turned around to face Chase. Behind Price, the koi's blue scales mixed with an aqueous cloud of blood. The piranha snapped its head back and forth, its slaughter creating a whirlpool of bubbles, which soon made the feeding frenzy unviewable.

"I'm sorry," Price said, returning to his desk, "you were saying."

Chase gulped. "I just wanted to stop in and pick up my check, since I'm going on vacation."

"Okey-dokey." Price opened a drawer and pulled out an envelope. "Here you go."

"Thanks," Chase said, making for the door.

He was almost there when Price asked, "Where you going?"

"Huh?"

"Where are you going on vacation?"

"Oh, back East. We have a little reunion to go to."

"That's right," Price said, clapping his hands once. "You

grew up in—what was it, Pittsburgh?"

"Philadelphia," Chase said.

"Right. The City of Brotherly Love, huh?"

Chase forced a smile. "That's what they tell me."

"Which airline are you taking?"

"Oh, we don't fly. Me and Monique were never too cracked up about flying, and after 9-11, we definitely don't want to hop on any airplane."

"It's not that bad."

"Probably not," Chase said, "but we don't mind driving. You get to see a lot on the road."

"But by the time you arrive for your reunion, it'll be time to leave."

"We'll have a good ten days out there. That's more than enough time to catch up with our family and friends."

"Right," Price said, snapping his fingers, "you're taking three weeks off."

"Mm-hmm. Well…um…uh, I guess I'll see you in three weeks."

"Have a safe trip."

"Thanks."

And with that, Chase closed his boss' office door and jogged through the warehouse to the parking lot.

CHAPTER 2

Chase slid into his Astro Van. It was colored maroon, except for the seats, which were black vinyl. The van was the only vehicle that he and Monique owned. Consequently, it served as an example of how their opposite personalities merged together into a happy medium. Chase was a self-admitted slob who shuddered at the mere mentioning of any type of housekeeping. Monique, meanwhile, was anal-retentive to the point of bordering on germ-freak status. These two polar personality traits resulted in the van being pleasurable for passengers to ride in. The van was clean but messy enough so it didn't feel like you were riding in a loaner from the car dealer lot.

Chase picked off the floor the half-full cup of soda he had gotten for lunch from the drive-thru at Wendy's. The ice had melted, but he didn't care, although he did cringe after the first slurp. Tasted syrupy.

Chase started the van. For a change, the engine turned over on the first try. The radio came to life. Punk rock blared, courtesy of the local college radio station. Chase shook his head. He couldn't believe he still listened to punk rock. Of course, the main reason it still entertained him was because one of his best friends from high school was a fervent fan of the genre. Not that there was anything wrong with that.

Chase placed his hand on the gearshift. He took the van out of park and meant to put it in drive but paused at neutral.

Why was his boss acting so cordial back there in the office? Usually, he never had a kind word to say about anyone or anything. In the three years Chase had worked here, he couldn't remember one time his boss had addressed him without using the word *moron*. Maybe his boss' behavior was a fluke, like Tom Hanks starring in a good movie. Or maybe his boss was experiencing the onset of a midlife crisis, and he'd finally realized what a jerk he'd been to his employees for the past fifteen years. (Part of his boss' modus operandi was to fire anybody who brought up the notion of a labor union.)

"Whatever," Chase said into the steering wheel, shifting the van into drive. He sipped on his warm soda and listened to NOFX sing about the libertarian plan. The Astro Van tore out of its parking spot.

CHAPTER 3

From his office, Pierce Price watched Chase Kilbey's Astro Van zip across his parking lot. Price had separated two slats of his venetian blinds to see which direction Kilbey was heading. The Astro Van idled at the parking lot exit, its left-rear turn signal blinking. Kilbey waited for a break in the four-lane avenue. After a couple minutes, an opening appeared. The Astro Van sputtered into the distance.

Price removed his index and middle fingers from separating the two venetian slats. He was glad to do so. The setting sun was beginning to hurt his eyes. Never mind that Kilbey's muffler rattled louder than the springs of a bed at the neighborhood whorehouse.

Price strode to his desk and picked up the phone. He hit speed dial, then the number 1.

"Hi, it's me," Price said into the phone. "No, I'm not calling from my cell. Yes, he just left. He's going back to Philadelphia for a 'little reunion.' Mm-hmm. That's what he said. Okay. B—"

Price didn't finish saying bye. His contact on the other end had disconnected.

CHAPTER 4

Monique Kilbey hosed down Macy, one of the African elephants here at the Anaheim Zoo. Macy made sure her large ears and long eyelashes received adequate H_2O treatment.

This was Monique's eighth year working at the zoo. She'd been here ever since she and Chase had moved to southern California in 1995 so Chase could pursue his dream of becoming a working character actor. When they first moved out here, Monique had a research job lined up at UCLA that sounded as if it was a step-up from the marine biologist position she had at the Trenton Aquarium in New Jersey. But when she and Chase arrived in Anaheim, there was suddenly no money budgeted for the position. It didn't take a college graduate to realize that was a lie. The man who had *hired* Monique, Mr. Feasly, flirted with her during the job interview, but she had thought nothing of it. Boys and men had been giving her preferential treatment for as long as she could remember. A long time ago, she'd made a conscious decision not to let it go to her head. She saw the devastating effect that flawless physical beauty had on her mother.

Growing up, Mrs. Flemming won countless beauty contests. She even won the Miss Universe pageant. But once middle age made its appearance, she fought every wrinkle and grey hair like a Roman soldier annihilating Christians. First, she started exercising more than Jane Fonda on a looped videotape. When that failed to halt the aging process, she invested in every makeup product the local super drugstore stocked. Then, at the age of thirty-five, she asked her husband for money so that she could afford plastic surgery. He refused, saying they had a mortgage, plus they needed to save for Monique's education. Mrs. Flemming begged for at least a nose job. Mr. Flemming still said no. Finally, one night at dinner, she said, "Either give me the goddamned money for the surgery, you selfish prick, or I'm divorcing you." Mr. Flemming jokingly pulled out the Yellow Pages from the china closet and opened it to the legal section. Mrs. Flemming whipped out a business card from her pocket and called a lawyer. Monique, ten years old at time, sat there shocked, jaw on her plate of chicken stir-fry. A year later, Monique's parents divorced. Immediately after the court proceedings, Mrs. Flemming landed a job as a salesperson, selling infomercials for local TV stations. She did get the plastic surgery she desperately desired, and soon initiated a string of affairs with Philadelphia-area bluebloods—some bachelors, but mostly married men. Monique lost track of her mother around her sixteenth birthday (when she transferred to another high school), but as a strange twist of fate, she'd recently discovered that her mother had remarried and was living in Beverly Hills.

"Monique!"

Monique snapped out of the trance the memories of her mother had put her in. She saw Charlene calling her from the roof of the Pachyderm House. Like Monique, Charlene was a zookeeper. Charlene had dark skin and black hair, an effect of her Cherokee ancestry.

"Can you wait another half-hour?" Charlene asked, hands cupped around her mouth like a megaphone.

"Sure," Monique answered. She and Charlene carpooled when they were on the same shift.

"Okay, thanks. Benjamin is being a real pain today." Benjamin was the western lowland gorilla that had arrived last week. He made it a point to sling dung at the zookeepers and bully his co-dwellers in the Primate House. "I'll meet you out by the car," Charlene said.

Monique gave Charlene a thumbs-up, then shut off the hose and turned to Macy. "Well, girl, you should be good to go."

Macy concurred by raising her trunk. The California sun shined off her dripping wet tusks.

Monique left the elephant yard, her boots and socks squishing.

CHAPTER 5

Monique opened her locker and grabbed from the top shelf a couple clean socks and an extra pair of boots. She kept at least one backup of each part of her uniform. She was glad she did so, especially on a day like today when her socks and boots seemed to get hosed more than Macy.

Wearing the dry socks and backup boots, Monique dropped the drenched socks and wet boots into a plastic 7-11 bag, which she placed in the tote bag she brought to work everyday.

Monique was about to close her locker when she saw that one of the Polaroids of Chase and her had untaped itself from inside the locker door. She picked the photo off the concrete floor. A feather clung to a corner of the pic. She blew it away and studied the Polaroid. It was from their vacation last year, from the week they spent hiking and camping in Yellowstone National Park. The photo showed them posing at daybreak in front of Old Faithful.

Monique placed the photo on the inside of her locker door, tucking the right edge of the pic into a slit on the side of the combination lock. She then closed the locker and walked down the long hallway to the parking lot.

This hallway always made Monique uncomfortable. Even though both sides had doors to offices and labs, it was still spookier than walking alone at night on a college campus. Maybe she didn't like this stretch of hallway because it was so dim. The only illumination came from twin-head floodlights that gave off a yellowish white hue.

Halfway down the hallway, Monique stopped quicker than you could say *Jumanji*. Why did she stop? She wasn't sure. It was…instinctual. Something deep inside her grey matter told her to halt.

Suddenly, one of the lab doors opened. Without hesitating, Monique slammed her back against the nearest wall. Her left

Johnny Ostentatious

shoulder hit a bulletin board. The board stayed intact, but a couple flyers fell off, their pushpins clicking to the ground like jacks. One of the flyers landed on her shoulder. A corner of it rested on her earlobe, just above her miniscule diamond earring; the flyer tickled her a little. Peripherally, she saw that it was red and made of heavy paper. Why was she able to see it so clearly? *Oh, jeez!* She was standing right in front of one of the few beams of light this hallway offered.

Out from the lab stepped two men, both wearing white knee-length lab coats. One of the men was about Monique's age—thirty-seven. He was lanky with a blond ponytail. The other man was much younger. Looked to be no older than twenty-five. He was of average build and height, and had black, curly hair. He wore fashionable eyeglasses, the kind with slim, oval frames.

"Dude," the twenty-five-year-old said in a New England accent, "we're going to be sooooo rich."

"We'll have to wait and see, man," said the partner in a mellow voice, the kind Monique associated with hippies.

Clutching her tote bag, Monique slid down the wall, out of the path of the light beam. The red flyer remained on her shoulder; the thought didn't occur to her to remove it. She was almost completely out of the light's path—only her feet were illuminated—when the flyer left her shoulder. She must have twitched without realizing it. *Damn!* The flyer flew over her head in an arc. She froze. It landed on her other shoulder. One of the flyer's edges tapped the knob of her shoulder, and since the flyer was made of heavy paper, it made the unmistakable sound of bending. Monique slid fully out of the light. The flyer began its *s-l-o-w* descent to the floor.

"What was that?" the New Englander said.

"What was what?" the hippie said.

"Didn't you hear it? Sounded like a sneak squeaking."

From her spot in the dark, Monique saw the hippie pinch the bridge of his nose.

"Look!" the New Englander said.

The flyer landed in the middle of the hallway. The New

Englander stared at the flyer, while the hippie massaged his own eyelids.

"Look," the New Englander said, "that's not the only flyer on the floor. There's a whole bunch of them. How'd that happen?"

"They probably fell off the bulletin board when you opened the door," the hippie said wearily.

"Hello," the New Englander called. "Anybody there?"

Monique gripped the handles of her tote bag. She prayed the smells of the animals on her weren't too potent.

"Come on, man," the hippie said, "let's go get a bite to eat."

"I heard something. I know I heard something."

"You're being paranoid, man. I told you to back off the coke, didn't I?"

"Somebody's here," the New Englander said. "I know it. They heard everything we said."

"But we didn't say anything, man," the hippie whined.

"You have the stun gun on you?"

The hippie sighed and nodded towards the lab door. "It's in there. Where we left it. Next to the…experiment."

The New Englander moved for the lab door. Monique felt a drop of sweat run across the back of her neck.

"Look, man," the hippie said, "you can go in there, get the stun gun and lurk up and down the hallway like a madman, but I'm going to the car and driving to McDonald's, then going home. We've been here for thirteen hours, man, and quite frankly, I'm exhausted."

"Just give me five minutes," the New Englander said.

"No." The hippie started down the hallway. Once within Monique's vicinity, he turned, still walking, and said, "I'll see you back at the house, man."

"All right, all right," the New Englander said, "you win." He jogged to catch up with his partner.

Monique pressed against the wall. The New Englander wasn't jogging down the center of the hallway. He was on the right side—the side where she hid in the shadows. If he bumped into her, who knew what would happen? She might be able to defend herself if there was only one of them, but she wouldn't be able to fend off both.

The New Englander jogged towards Monique, his arms swinging wildly. She tensed up. The New Englander reached her. His elbow just missed her, but the bottom corner of his lab coat brushed her knee. Monique gasped. The New Englander stopped jogging. He turned.

"You coming?" the hippie said from the mouth of the hallway.

The New Englander stepped towards Monique. She saw him as a silhouette. He reached into one of his lab coat pockets. Out came a scalpel. He held it at chest level. For a second, the blade glinted.

"Hope you enjoy taking the bus back to Cypress, man" the hippie called, his voice faint. *He must be in the parking lot*, Monique thought.

"Fuck it," the New Englander mumbled. He deposited the scalpel back into his pocket and resumed his jog down the hallway, his footsteps echoing.

Once the New Englander was completely out of sight, Monique exhaled loudly and dropped her bag. Her legs felt as if they were filled with Jell-O. She could have collapsed to the ground but resisted the urge. Instead, she marched across the hall to the lab door that the hippie and the New Englander had exited.

CHAPTER 6

The door was unlocked. The New Englander had been so intent on locating Monique that he and the hippie had forgotten to lock the door. Monique smiled at their carelessness, while stepping into the lab, closing the door behind her, dropping her tote bag and turning on the light.

The lab was small compared to the other ones Monique had seen at the zoo. On the left were supplies jammed in metal cabinets with glass doors, and on the right was a black marble table. The space between the cabinets and table was barely wide enough for one slender researcher, let alone two of average bulk.

Monique shrieked.

On the marble table lay a baby harp seal. Around its *neck* was a leather collar. Attached to the collar was a chain. The end of the chain looped around an iron ring screwed into the wall.

"Oh my God!" Monique said, hands over mouth.

The seal looked up at Monique with droopy, glassy eyes.

"What have they done to you?"

Monique petted the seal's head. It leaned sideways in an effort to nestle against her, but the chain was too short. Monique unbuckled the collar. The seal undulated towards her. She stroked its short, white fur, then stopped.

At the end of the table was a closed laptop. Monique opened it, finding it had been left on. Again, the hippie and New Englander's carelessness amazed her.

The only program open on the computer was Microsoft Word, with a log that detailed the hippie and New Englander's experiment. They had injected the harp seal with a serum that rose its body temperature, letting the seal inhabit any climate, not strictly arctic ones. Monique saw how an experiment like this could make the hippie and the New Englander wealthy. With the serum, southern California zoos could display wintry animals without worrying about recreating frigid, glacial conditions, saving zoos millions of dollars. Monique frowned. She wondered how many seals the hippie and New Englander had murdered in their quest for fame and affluence.

A rage filled Monique. She swiped the laptop off the table and rose it above her head. She was about to hurl it to the floor when a better idea hit her. She placed the laptop back on the table, then grabbed a lab stool, sat on it and began deleting all of the computer's files. Afterwards, she emptied the recycle bin and reformatted the hard drive, guaranteeing that the hippie and New Englander couldn't bring up any files associated with "the experiment." Next, she searched the room for any hard copies of their data. She didn't find anything. They must have done everything electronically.

By this point, the seal had worked its way off the table. It rolled around on the floor, clapping its flippers.

"Well, kid," Monique said, "it looks like my work is done here. Do you need a ride?"

The seal barked.

Monique picked up her tote bag. "Let's go find Charlene, then."

CHAPTER 7

Chase opened the door to the apartment he and Monique had called home for the past five years.

"Hon, you here?"

"In the bathroom," Monique answered.

Chase deadbolted the door and tossed his keys and wallet into the glass bowl next to the door. He and Monique always put their valuables in this bowl. Monique had created it back in high school for her craft class. Painted on the bowl, in fluorescent green, were seven infinity symbols linked together to form a chain.

Next to the infinity bowl was the day's mail. Chase fanned through it. Nothing but bills and junk mail. He dropped it into the bowl, which sat on a waist-high end table. At the foot of the table was a rack that held magazines, catalogs and phone books. Chase and Monique had bought the table, like most of their furniture, at a yard sale.

Chase and Monique loved yard sales. They couldn't get enough of them. They were such yard sale aficionados that they would drive out of state if one was advertised heavily on the Internet. Friends and acquaintances often asked Chase and Monique why they were such ardent yard sale patrons. Chase would joke that they were forced to be frugal "'cause we gots no money," while Monique would answer seriously that it was a resonance of their working-class roots.

Chase walked through the living room. He passed the kitchen on the left. The smell of last night's supper, shrimp scampi, hung in the air. *Better take the trash out tonight, or the rats'll be back*, he thought.

Chase headed down the hallway that led to the bedroom. Halfway there, he stopped to open the bathroom door.

"Hey," Chase asked, "how we looking on packing?"

"Pretty good," Monique answered.

Johnny Ostentatious

She was sitting on the floor in front of the bathtub, her back to Chase. Her auburn, permed hair was up in a bun, exposing her slender neck. Chase was about to kneel down and kiss that alluring neck, when he saw it.

A harp seal peeked over Monique's shoulder. Chase knew it sounded crazy, but he swore it was smiling at him.

Monique turned around. "Chase, meet Spanky. Spanky, Chase."

Spanky barked. Monique dropped her hand into the tub (it was half-full), cupped some water in her palm and poured it over Spanky's head. The seal closed its eyes in delight, then splashed around.

"Where did *that* come from?" Chase asked.

"That is Spanky. I found him at the zoo."

"What, they were giving them away?"

"Not exactly," Monique said.

"Well, what exactly?"

Monique told him. After she finished, Chase asked, "Won't they know you took this…er…um…Spanky? I mean, won't those two guys go to the zoo, tell them what happened, then the zoo'll do a search and find your fingerprints all over the lab?"

"I don't think so. I seriously doubt that that hippie and New Englander were sanctioned by the zoo. I can't see the zoo funding that sort of research. They're pretty conservative."

"Okay, but once they find out their seal's missing, even if they don't go looking for it, won't they have backup files of the stuff you deleted?"

"I've already thought about that and have made sure they never hurt any other animals again."

"How's that?" Chase asked.

"I called the American Medical Association, the SPCA and the zoo's front office, and left anonymous messages on their voicemails. One of them should be able to put those two scientist creeps out of commission. And just in case that doesn't work, I called Paula Garrett."

"Paula Garrett?"

"She's the one on Channel Five that does those exposés on cruelty to animals."

"Those guys'll get arrested for sure."

"I hope so," Monique said.

By now, Chase was sitting on the edge of the tub. He touched Monique's cheek and tucked a curl of her hair behind her ear. She smiled.

"So," Chase said, "who's watching the old Spankster while we go back to Philly?"

"Oh, he's coming with us."

"What!"

Monique shrugged angelically.

"No," Chase said. "No way is it coming with us."

"He's not an it. His name's Spanky."

"Hon, think about it. Taking him with us isn't practical. How's he going to survive a 3,000-mile road trip in our van? He could die."

"He'll be fine," Monique said. "He survived all the poking and prodding by those two demonic researchers. Why shouldn't he be fine in the van?"

"But even though he has that serum pumping through him, he's still a seal. He's going to need water and other seal stuff like that."

"He'll be fine. We'll bring along the steel washtub we got at that yard sale last month. He can swim around in that."

"What about food?" Chase asked.

"What about it? They'll be plenty of places to stop on the way."

"How do we know the serum won't wear off? We could get to Philly and have him get sick or something."

"Stop worrying," Monique said. "We'll be fine."

"Who's going to take care of him when we finally get to Philly? We're going to be pretty busy, you know."

"I know. My dad can take care of him."

Chase, still sitting on the edge of the tub, let loose a curt laugh. "You've thought of everything, haven't you?"

"It's like you always say," Monique said, "where there's a will, there's a Kilbey."

As if sensing Chase still had some reservations, Spanky rested his head on Chase's hip and placed a flipper on his thigh.

"Well?" Monique said pleasantly.

Chase glanced at Spanky's Bambi eyes.

"All right," Chase said, "he can go."

CHAPTER 8

The next morning, Chase and Monique packed up their Astro Van. It didn't take long. They were light packers.

The washtub was the last item they placed in the van. The tub was oval, galvanized and could hold sixteen gallons. The bottom had two ridges in the shape of circles, one encircling the other. Specs of rust flaked from the tub's handles. There was no other rust in or on the tub, so it had no holes.

Chase was strapping the tub into the rear corner of the van, on the passenger side, when Spanky hopped into the tub. Chase couldn't help but laugh.

Soon, Monique returned from the beer distributor with two bags of ice. Chase slit the bags with his Swiss army knife and dumped the ice into the tub. Spanky rolled around like Winnie the Pooh in a vat of honey.

"You sure this is all necessary?" Chase asked Monique. "I mean, since they injected him with all that serum, shouldn't he not need ice or anything cold?"

"Oh, he doesn't *need* it," Monique said. "That was made abundantly clear by the log that hippie and New Englander had on their laptop, but it'll make him happy."

"Who, you or Spanky?"

"Spanky," Monique said seriously. "If you were him, wouldn't you like to have a corner you could go and lounge in?"

"Sort of like a spa, huh?" Chase said with a smirk.

"Like but not quite," Monique said, smirking back.

CHAPTER 9

Three days later, Monique and Chase were more than halfway to Philadelphia. They were riding through Des Moines, Iowa, with Monique at the wheel. Before leaving Anaheim, Monique and Chase had planned out a daily schedule for their trip. They would wake up at 6:00 A.M., hop in the van and stop at the first convenience store they saw to buy milk for the box of Raisin Bran they'd brought along for the trip. After breakfast, they'd drive for six hours, then stop at a deli. After lunch, they'd drive for three or four more hours until they found a place to crash. Most nights, they parked at a camping ground, in a mall parking lot or on the side street of a quiet residential area. Every third night, they stayed at a motel in order to sleep on a mattress, instead of in the back of the van. Monique looked forward to the motel stays. Not because of the comfort, but because of the showers. She and Chase would take half-hour showers in warm water. The showers were extremely erotic. After washing each other, they did things to each other that would make Hugh Hefner blush. Monique was getting excited just thinking about it. She pushed it out of her mind by focusing on the farm truck in front of them. It had hay and corn stalks piled six feet high.

Monique and Chase were now passing through the center of Des Moines. Buildings housing insurance companies loomed on either side of the avenue. The sun was setting. The purple horizon slowly turned black.

"Oh, boy," Monique said.

She tapped the brakes. Up ahead, construction closed off one lane of traffic. Monique brought the Astro Van to a stop. It idled under a skywalk. Shade from the skywalk shadowed the inside of the van. Monique glanced at Chase. She could hardly see him due to a combination of the skywalk shade and the headlights of the truck behind them glaring off the Astro Van's passenger-side mirror.

"I've been thinking," Chase said.

"What about?" Monique asked.

"This trip."

Monique heard Chase crack his knuckles. The traffic started moving. The Astro Van crept out of the shade of the skywalk. Monique saw Chase's fingers fidget.

"Things really need to work out for us," Chase said. "I can't go back to working for that prick Price."

"You can always get another job."

"What's the point? All it'll be is another bottom-rung gig with crappy pay and a boss I can't stand."

"I know," Monique said.

"I just hope everything goes smoothly when we get out there."

"I don't see why it shouldn't."

"You never know," Chase said, "Murphy's Law might be in full effect. That seems to happen a lot with simple plans—things get complicated."

"We'll have to wait and see," Monique said.

Chase nodded. The traffic started moving a hair faster than a snail's pace. The Astro Van left the shadiness of the skywalk. Monique rolled down her window. She smelled horse manure from the farm truck in front of her. She rolled the window back up.

Chase sighed and shifted towards Monique. "I just wish I could make a living at acting."

"I know, but we gave it a shot. How many aspiring actors can say that? Most only hang around their non-show biz town and whine about how they were never discovered. At least we moved all the way to the other side of the country to give you the best chance to pursue your dream."

"True."

In 1995, when Monique had moved out to California with Chase, they had been married for three years. The deal she made with him was that she would support him for five years while he tried to make it as an actor. She believed the odds were in his favor. After all, for the last few years they'd lived in Philadelphia, Chase had steady acting jobs in theater and independent movies. Most of them paid poorly or—in the case of indie movies—not at all; however, during their last year in Philly, Chase had netted $10,000 from his acting endeavors. Not enough to live on, but enough so that he only had to supplement his income with a ten-hour-a-week construction job. But despite all of that, Chase failed to slip his foot into the Hollywood door. He only got his big toe in by working in commercials and getting the occasional walk-on in a sitcom. Monique was just as disappointed as Chase when the five-year deadline arrived in June of 2000.

Chase opened the Astro Van's glovebox and removed a stick of gum from the supersize Wrigley pack they had picked up this afternoon at Flo's Deli. Chase asked Monique if she wanted a stick. She said yes. When passing it off, his wedding ring grazed her palm. It tickled a little. She smiled at him.

"Do you ever regret moving out to California?" Chase asked.

"Why would I regret it?" Monique asked.

"You had a pretty sweet deal back in Philly—nice job, good friends, decent house...great marriage." He smirked on the *great marriage* part. "That was a lot to give up to move 3,000 miles away to the land of celluloid dreams."

"I don't think so. You wanted to move to L.A.; I thought about it and said yes. And it's not like I said yes right away. Remember, I took a couple weeks to think about it."

Chase nodded.

Monique continued, "If I was even a little bit reluctant, I would've said no, and we would've worked something out. But there hasn't been a day that's gone by that I regretted it."

"Even though what you're doing now doesn't require a biology degree?"

"I don't mind it. In fact, some days I actually enjoy working at the zoo. Some of those animals are smarter and kinder than some people I know."

"I just feel like a bit of a failure," Chase said.

"You shouldn't." Monique hit the gas to cut around the road construction. "Why should you feel like a failure? So what if you didn't make it as an actor. Didn't you tell me before that only one percent of all actors are gainfully employed?"

"Yeah, but—"

"That's some pretty high odds. Sounds like you'd have better chances winning the lottery."

"I know."

"Besides," Monique said, "we still have each other."

Chase grinned. "That's true."

"And I would like to think that if the roles were reversed, you would've moved thousands of miles for me."

"Of course," Chase said without hesitation.

"I love you, Chase."

"I love you, too, hon."

And with that, the Astro Van drove through the rest of Des Moines. Monique was looking forward to their stay in a motel tonight.

CHAPTER 10

A half-mile behind Chase and Monique rode Pierce Price. He had been tailing the Astro Van in his Mitsubishi Spyder ever since they left California.

Price was glad Kilbey used his Astro Van for this cross-country trip. It was easy to tail with the stickers plastered on the bumper and rear doors. Half of the stickers were names of punk-rock bands, while the other half were slogans from bleeding-heart organizations like Greenpeace, Food Not Bombs and Books Through Bars.

Price lit a cigarette. Even though the Astro Van was easy to tail, he wished Kilbey had taken a plane. That would've worked out well for Price. He could've racked up some frequent-flyer miles. But no, Kilbey and his wife had to travel by van. *Simpletons.*

Price still thought trailing Kilbey was overkill, but Price's contact in Philadelphia insisted that the Astro Van never leave his sight. Price reluctantly obeyed orders. Hopefully, when they reached Philadelphia, the aggravation of the 3,000-mile trek would be worth it.

CHAPTER 11

Thirty-six-year-old Nick Marsh was a gangly punk rocker with huge biceps and veiny forearms. Reason why his arms were so hardcore? Nick got into more fights than Don King.

Nick loved to fight. It was in his blood. His father and five brothers were fighters. At an early age, Nick's dad had drilled into the Marsh boys that a fight was the only way to get your point across.

Nick had gotten into a fight last night. At a bar, a yuppie cut in front of him, so Nick did what any self-respecting Philadelphian would do. He grabbed the yuppie by the tie and yanked it down. The yuppie's head bounced off the bar so hard, wood chips went flying. When the yuppie's head came back up, Nick kicked him into the corner, where the yuppie collapsed into the unconsciousness.

Why?

That was the question Nick constantly asked himself. Why did he feel the need to get into a fight at the drop of a drink? The answer was obvious. He was a small guy: five-two. Fighting was his way of showing the world he wasn't going to be stepped on or pushed around. He first became aware of this motivation eleven years ago, at the age of twenty-five, but the frequency of his fighting was the same now as it had been when he was a teenager. What could he do? It was in his blood. After all, his father had boxed professionally in the 1950s on weekends in Atlantic City casinos.

Currently, Nick was in Chicago. He was onstage, playing bass for the punk band Farting Out A Fetus, or FOAF as their small but devout legion of fans called them. FOAF was three-quarters through their half-hour set. They played for a crowd of two hundred in a church basement at an all-ages show. *It's hotter down here than the gas coming out of my ass*, Nick thought.

Nick stood in his usual onstage position, to the right of Dave the drummer. Nick wore the same outfit he'd been sporting since junior high. Black Chuck Taylor high-tops, blue jeans, white T-shirt and a choker chain necklace with a little combination lock hanging above his manubrium.

Nick's bass solo was coming up. He built up to it, riding a G chord as Dave beat the bass drum and pounded the floor tom. Nick stepped up to center stage. FOAF's two guitarists moved aside and stopped playing. Time for the bass solo. Nick ripped into it. The solo lasted only five seconds, but in the hyperkinetic world of punk rock, that was an eon. Nick finished the solo as he had every other night of FOAF's six-week tour. He strode back to his spot next to Dave's floor tom and struck the last note of the solo while stamping on an effects pedal. The pedal gave the note a reverb-ish effect. As the reverb faded, FOAF's two guitarists returned to center stage and began playing again, their power chords louder than a train crash.

The song ended. FOAF ripped into their next song, a thirty-second ditty called "Profit." Nick played it with his eyes closed. "Profit" was FOAF's oldest song—five years. It was the first tune Nick had learned to play for the band when he joined nine months ago.

Nick wasn't so much a member of FOAF as a hired hand. He shared no songwriting credit and had no say in touring or business decisions, which suited him fine. He'd been in bands before where every member pulled their weight creatively and manage-rially, but that usually led to bickering and the inevitable breakup. Nick enjoyed played in FOAF. It was refreshing to be follower instead of a leader. Although, Nick knew eventually he would get the itch to book his own life again. Until then, he would enjoy this setup, his version of a vacation.

FOAF paused between songs to allow the lead guitarist to tune his Les Paul. The rhythm guitarist, the band's vocalist, bantered to the audience. Nick glanced at his watch on his left wrist. The watch was part of a three-inch-wide leather wristband; spike studs encircled the watch. It was 10:45 P.M. They had to be off the stage in fifteen minutes. Since this was an all-ages show,

Noir Reunion

they had to be mindful of curfew.

The lead guitarist was still tuning his Les Paul. Nick studied the audience. They stared at the band, waiting patiently. Except one audience member. In the back of the basement, a fourteen-year-old girl leaned against the wall, attention fixed on her PalmPilot.

The lead guitarist finally finished tuning his Les Paul. Immediately, FOAF ripped into the first of their last three songs. Towards the end of the two-minute tune, Nick began missing notes. It wasn't because of inebriation or any other musician cliché. Rather, it was because his attention was elsewhere. Namely, on the fourteen-year-old with the PalmPilot.

A nineteen-year-old meathead had cornered the fourteen-year-old in the back of the basement. She tried escaping, but he blocked her path. Nobody in the audience noticed. Their eyes were on FOAF.

Nick yelled and pointed but no audience members turned to look in the back. They must have thought he was acting goofy as part of the show.

The meathead was now taunting the girl. He tapped her ear, poked her waist and grabbed her breasts. He did each action one at a time, so as she went to cover her breasts, his other hand tapped her ear, forcing her to move her hands to her head, leaving her waist and breasts open for the next poke or grab. In the process of protecting herself, she dropped her PalmPilot. It fell to the floor. Nick heard no clacking. How could he? FOAF's music drowned everything out.

Nick made another attempt to let the audience know what was happening. He didn't have a microphone of his own, so he stepped towards the lead guitarist's. But the guitarist, his back to Nick, was shouting backup vocals into the mike. Nick thought of pushing him aside but decided not to—too much trouble. Nick stopped playing his bass. The rest of the band didn't notice. They were caught up in the moment of the music, especially Dave the drummer, his eyes closed.

"Fuck this," Nick mumbled.

Johnny Ostentatious

He threw his bass down. It crashed into the amp, creating feedback only a mute could love.

Nick dove into the crowd. They cheered, slapping his back. Next thing Nick knew, he was bodysurfing across the crowd.

"Put me down," Nick yelled. "Put me down, you assholes!"

Apparently, they didn't hear him. They held him above their heads with their hands and arms, bodysurfing him every which way but down to the ground. *Well,* Nick thought, *if they aren't gonna put me down, I might as well* surf *to the back of the basement.* In order to do so, he was going to have to turn over. Up until this point, he'd been bodysurfing facedown.

Nick turned over and moved his arms and legs as if he was sitting on his butt and meant to scuttle forward. The crowd got the message. They surfed him towards the back of the basement. It wasn't pretty, though. Nick felt long nails inadvertently dig into his back; his wallet chain snagged a couple people's headgear; and since this was a punk-rock show, a few bad asses punched him. The punches landed on his shoulders and didn't hurt much. After all, throwing a fist against gravity lacks force.

Halfway to the back of the basement, the crowd let Nick down. He landed on his feet, like a veteran superhero. *That's me, Punk-Rock Man. Where's my cape?*

Nick sprinted towards the back of the basement. Humid air zipped past his head. He prayed he wasn't too late.

Not bothering to slow his sprint down, Nick ran into the meathead. He bounced off the meathead's back as if it was made of rubber. Nick landed on the steps that led up to the bathroom. To pull himself up, he reached for the cool hollow metal railing. While doing this, he kept his eyes on the raping in the making. The girl's eyes reminded him of a frightened rabbit that knew a clobbering was imminent.

"Hey!" Nick said.

The meathead turned slightly. Up close, Nick saw that the meathead was built like a refrigerator with a head the shape of an anvil.

"Take a hike, little man," the meathead said in a Mike Tyson voice.

"Hey," Nick said again. He tried pushing the meathead away from the girl but couldn't. The meathead's arm seemed to consist of cast iron.

The girl's bunny eyes pleaded with Nick, tears clouding her green irises.

"Hey, Brutus," Nick said. "Why don't you pick on someone from your own species, say an ape."

After the word *ape* left Nick's mouth, he saw a flash of light and heard the crack of a whip. Next thing he knew, he was lying on the floor. What just happened? The question was rhetorical. The meathead had hit Nick with such quickness and force that he was on his back before his brain could register it all.

Nick sat up. Nausea caused him to sway. Ignoring his stomach's threat to hurl, he reached for his wallet chain. He unhooked it from his belt loop and wallet. The chain measured two feet. Nick held it, a hand at each end. He pulled it taut.

Nick jumped on the meathead's back. The meathead didn't stagger a centimeter. Nick wrapped his legs around the meathead's waist and threw his arms over the wannabe rapist's head.

The meathead torpedoed his hands towards Nick. Nick cringed. The meathead's hands—bigger than boxing gloves—tried grasping Nick's hair, but fortunately he shaved his head monthly, his hair never growing more than a quarter-inch.

The meathead grunted and growled. Since latching onto Nick's hair wasn't an option, the meathead shifted strategy by grabbing for the ears. Nick swerved his head away from the meathead's hands, which wasn't easy because the goon's hairy arms kept distracting him.

The meathead then tried throwing Nick off his back. Nick held on and realized two things: he wasn't aware if FOAF still played, and he hadn't used the wallet chain yet. No time to worry about FOAF, but he could address the second point.

Nick wrapped the chain around the meathead's neck. The chain barely made it all the way around.

The meathead yelled like a Viking rushing into battle. He

stomped back and forth. Nick held on by squeezing the wallet chain, which proved increasingly difficult. His sweaty palms kept sliding towards the ends of the chain.

The meathead stopped stomping around. He bent over, hands on knees.

Uh-oh, Nick thought. *What's he doing?*

The meathead remained in that position for about ten seconds. Nick took the time to glance around. FOAF had stopped playing. The band and the audience gaped at Nick and the meathead.

Nick sensed the meathead's breathing returning to normal. Nick held onto the wallet chain. It wasn't choking the meathead, but it was tight enough to be labeled uncomfortable.

"You gonna die," the meathead gargled.

"What's that, horsy?"

Nick had barely gotten his comeback out when the meathead broke into a run. Nick held on. The meathead, yelling, ran in a circle. Nick shut his eyes. Everything zipping by made him dizzy. Suddenly, the meathead changed course. A half moment later, the running came to a grinding halt. Nick's eyes popped open. The meathead slammed Nick's back against a wall. Nick's body, starting with the base of his spine, absorbed the shock of the slam. His body quivered.

"Ugh," Nick said.

He let go of the wallet chain and slid down the meathead's back. But the meathead wasn't going to let Nick fall to the floor. He gripped the punk rocker by the ears. This time, Nick didn't have the energy to swerve away. The meathead gripped Nick's ears in a specific way, as if this wasn't a new scenario to him. The meathead placed his fingers behind Nick's ears and inserted his thumbs into the punk rocker's ear canals, as far as they would go. Nick screamed. The meathead's thumbs pushed up inside the canals. Simultaneously, the meathead's fingers dug into the back of Nick's ears. Nick couldn't see. He told himself his eyes were watering, not tearing. He then wondered if the ear pain could get any worse. As an answer, the meathead moved his thumbs and fingers to get a firmer grip, then slammed Nick's forehead against the back of his head. Nick saw stars in his peripheral vision. He fell backwards and hung upside down, his legs still wrapped around the meathead's waist.

"Get the fuck off me, faggot!"

The meathead's words echoed inside Nick's head. He was having trouble concentrating. His scalp was brushing the sticky basement floor. He felt the meathead's he-man hands on his ankles in an attempt to unlock them from around his waist. That's when Nick saw it. The wallet chain hung from his wristband; two of the spike studs pinched together, the wallet chain its captive. Nick fought the grogginess the fight had induced. His right hand snatched the chain. The movement made his back crack, but he ignored it. Payback time.

Tightening his stomach muscles, Nick performed the hardest sit-up of his life. Halfway up, he didn't like what was happening. The meathead was unlocking Nick's ankles from around his waist. Nick gasped. He began descending. With what little energy he had left, he reached ceilingward, threw his hands over the meathead's skull and wrapped the chain around his neck again. The meathead's huge hands searched for Nick's ears. Nick ducked and pulled on the chain. It slid up and over the meathead's Adam's apple. The meathead dropped to his knees with such a thud, Nick wondered if the entire building shook. *Never mind that.* Nick gave the chain a tug Batman would have been proud of. That collapsed the meathead to one side, like a lumbering brontosaurus. Nick hopped off of him. He looked up.

The band and the crowd gawked at him. Nick blocked them out, as he had for most of the fight. He sauntered around the meathead, who lied on his right side, arm covering face. Nick's foot tapped the meathead's chest. The arm flopped off his face.

"Fucker," Nick said. He kicked the meathead, steadily increasingly his rhythm, his arms stretching out horizontally. Each kick crept lower down the meathead's body. Eventually, Nick reached the groin. That's when he felt a tugging on his drenched T-shirt. He turned. It was the fourteen-year-old girl.

"Please," she said. "Don't kill him. I don't want you to go to prison."

Nick nodded. He gave the meathead one final kick.

CHAPTER 12

Chase and Monique pulled the Astro Van over to the shoulder on I-95. They hopped out and stood several feet in front of the van, watching steam billow through the grille.

"Do you believe this?" Chase said, laughing.

Monique shook her head. She removed her Jackie O sunglasses and stepped back. The overheating Astro Van was smothering her.

"I can't believe our luck," Chase said, giggling. "I mean, the van's fine for 3,000 miles, then boom! We're not two miles from your dad's house, and it overheats. Do we rule or what?"

Monique nodded, only catching half of what Chase said, thanks to the roaring by of six lanes of expressway traffic. Despite only hearing some of what he said, she wasn't amused. She had done much of the driving over the past five days. She was more exhausted than Shamu after entertaining crowds all day at Seaworld.

Anytime Monique and Chase traveled somewhere—whether it was a party or a vacation—she did most of the driving. Not that she minded. She loved driving. It filled her with a sense of freedom. Just her and the open road. And if any vehicles in front of her went slower than ten miles over the speed limit, watch out. She had no qualms with zooming past slowpokes, whether there was a passing lane or not.

The Astro Van was beginning to cool down. It was still overheated, but not so much that it appeared like the Detroit version of a brushfire.

Monique put her sunglasses back on. She leaned against the guardrail and looked down at State Road. Traffic was heavy on the four lanes. Across the street, factories and strip bars littered the landscape that butted against the Delaware River. One of the strip bars, Cloud 9, used to be an arts-and-crafts store called Kay's Place. As a teenager, Monique spent many allowances and paychecks there.

"What do you want to do?" Chase asked.

"Might as well start walking," Monique answered.

"What about the Spankster?"

"Let's take him with us."

They opened the rear doors of the van. An eager Spanky, lounging in the washtub, greeted them. Monique petted him on the head, then pulled out a red wagon—another one of their yard-sale treasures. Chase picked up Spanky and placed him in the wagon. Before closing the van doors, Monique dumped some ice from the tub into the wagon.

Monique pulled the wagon. Spanky wasn't too heavy.

"Hon," Monique said to Chase, "can you walk on the left so Spanky doesn't jump into the traffic?"

Chase did, but it turned out to be unnecessary. The traffic zooming by scared Spanky. He crouched down in the wagon, flippers covering his head.

Spanky didn't cower for too long, though. The Astro Van had broken down two hundred yards from the Cottman Avenue exit in Northeast Philadelphia. Soon, they were off the shoulder of I-95 and walking up Cottman Ave.

It amazed Monique how little Cottman Ave had changed in the years she'd been away. When you first got off the I-95 ramp, the area was more industrial than residential. But once you crossed Torresdale Avenue, with the Septa depot on the left and Saint Hubert's High School for Girls on the right, you entered a residential area, row homes lining both sides of the avenue.

It felt weird to walk up Cottman Ave. Monique couldn't remember the last time she'd strolled up or down it. In the Philly borough they were now in, Mayfair, nobody walked more than a quarter-mile. Anything over that and you drove. If you were underage, you got a ride, usually from a family member. Monique's father had chauffeured her around until she got her license on her sixteenth birthday. He didn't mind carting her around for those fifteen years. In fact, she was pretty sure he enjoyed it. Why else was he always on time and never argumentative if she was late (unless she missed curfew)?

Monique looked down at Spanky. He was much more relaxed now that they had put considerable distance between themselves and I-95. Spanky was rolling around in what little ice was in the wagon. Every block or so, he would stop and turn his attention to a dog in a front yard that was barking at him. Spanky would raise a fin, as if a celebrity recognizing a vocal fan. The first time Spanky did this, Monique laughed.

"What?" Chase asked.

Monique told him.

"Yeah," Chase said, "I gotta admit: that's one cool seal."

"Aren't you glad we brought him?"

"Maybe," Chase said, smirking.

They came to Bleigh Street and made a left. Monique's father lived halfway down the block.

Like the other row homes on the block, the front of the house Monique grew up in had a short flight of concrete steps, then an open porch, and another short flight of steps, which led to the front door. The porch had a lawn, a barbecue grill, an umbrella table and two white lawn chairs. Monique sat in one of the chairs. She took off her sandals and rested her feet on the lawn; a patch of crabgrass tickled the arch of her left foot. She noticed her father's porch was the only one on the block that still had a lawn. Everyone else had replaced theirs with slabs of cement. Made sense. This was the city, not the country.

While Monique tilted back in the lawn chair, Chase knocked on the front door.

"Doesn't look like he's home," Chase said.

"It's almost four. He should be here soon."

Monique's father worked as an electrician at the University of Pennsylvania. His hours were from 7:00 A.M. to 3:30 P.M. She knew he enjoyed that shift because it gave him the time to moonlight with his steady stream of under-the-table side jobs. The side jobs had been especially plentiful after Monique's mom divorced him. Good thing, too. Alimony for the first few years was substantial. Without the side jobs, Monique and her dad would have gone bankrupt. And if that happened, Monique's mom would have demanded the court tack on astronomical interest to the deferred alimony.

Chase sat in a lawn chair next to Monique. "Hey," he said, "guess what?"

"What?"

"I'm having flashbacks of when we first started dating."

"Oh, yeah?"

"What do you say we relive those days of yore by making out like hormone-overloaded teenagers?"

"In broad daylight?" Monique said, smiling.

"Who's going to see? Come on, it's Bleigh Street. Everybody's at work or watching *Oprah*."

"Not *Doctor Phil*?"

"Nobody watches *Doctor Phil*," Chase said. "Even Doctor Phil's family and friends don't watch *Doctor Phil*."

"That bad, huh?"

"The worst. He gives head jobs a bad name." Chase slid out of his chair to kneel next to Monique.

Monique felt Chase's soft lips press against hers. She didn't know why it was, but his kisses aroused her now as much as they did when they made out on this porch twenty years ago. Each time they kissed or made love, Monique treated it as if it were their last. You never knew if one of you were going to die tomorrow, or worse, become bored with the relationship.

Monique heard a car door slam. She broke the kiss and saw her father's stocky frame standing on the sidewalk at the foot of the steps.

Grinning, he pointed at Spanky. "What the hell is that?"

CHAPTER 13

With their six-week tour complete, Farting Out A Fetus returned to Philadelphia. The band dropped Nick off at his apartment in the Spring Garden section of the city.

Nick lugged up the stairs his duffel bag full of dirty clothes. He also carried his bass, but that didn't slow him down because he didn't own a case for it—he simply threw it over his back, like a rifle. And, thankfully, he didn't have to drag his amp up the steps. He kept it at Dave the drummer's house, where FOAF (when not touring or recording) practiced three times a week.

Nick finally reached the floor he lived on, the eighth. He paused to catch his breath and remembered the reservations he'd had five years ago when he moved in here with his boyfriend, David. *Shouldn't they have a elevator here?* Nick had asked. David shrugged and smirked, as only he could. David didn't mind the stairs. At that point, he had been living here for two years.

Nick dragged himself down the hall to the apartment. Still a bit winded from climbing the steps, he stopped a couple times. *Gotta quit smoking.*

Key in hand, Nick noticed the door to the apartment was ajar. Shrugging, he walked in.

The apartment was quaint but cozy: hardwood floors, stucco ceiling and walls painted fuchsia blue.

Nick dropped his bass and duffel bag next to the loveseat. He went to the kitchen and opened the refrigerator.

"Nice."

There was still a twelve-pack of Budweiser in the crisper. Nick had bought it before he went on tour. David never drank beer. He preferred wine.

Sipping his Bud, Nick walked through the apartment.

"Babe, you here?"

Nick reached the bedroom door. It was closed. Dance music

rattled from behind it. David was probably exercising. They kept their Nordic Track in there.

Nick opened the door. He was going to surprise his partner by saying *boo*, but all that came out was "Buh."

Nick couldn't believe what he was witnessing. He dropped his beer. It landed on his left Chuck Taylor, tipped over and spilled into his sock. Once empty, the can fell off his sneak, clanging, and rolled across the floor towards the bed.

The room reeked of sweat and Vaseline.

David, Nick's lover of eight years, sat on the bed, fucking a twenty-year-old. The twink wore a cowboy hat. *A cowboy in Philadelphia?* Nick managed to think through the shock.

A wave of dizziness overcame Nick. He staggered. His beer-soaked sock squished. The dance music thumped. Nick had always hated dance music. And this was the worst. Techno. More specifically, jungle.

David, eyes closed, continued to hump the cowboy doggie-style. Nick covered his mouth with his hand, tears clouding his vision.

Suddenly, David's eyes popped open. It wasn't because he sensed Nick's proximity. No, David always opened his eyes when he came.

The cowboy smirked at Nick, his eyes and nose shaded by the rim of his ten-gallon hat.

David looked away from Nick as he finished his orgasm. He pulled out of the cowboy and collapsed onto the bed. Nick gaped. David wasn't wearing a condom. Nick's stomach rumbled. In their eight years together, how many times had David had unprotected sex with other men?

Nick stormed out of the room. He knew it made him look like a drama queen, but he couldn't stay here. The sight of David naked still got him hard. Nick knew it shouldn't, but David's blond hair, chiseled-cut chin and muscular chest still turned him on.

Nick stamped into the kitchen. He tossed the remainder of his Budweiser twelve-pack into the duffel bag and slung his bass over his shoulder. He was so out of here. He had no choice, really. This was David's apartment. For the past five years, David's income as a stockbroker had been supporting Nick's musical career.

Nick opened the front door of the apartment. Letting go of the doorknob, he tapped his hand against his hip and idled in the doorway, waiting to see if David would rush out, begging for forgiveness.

David didn't. Nick heard giggling from the bedroom.

"Do it again, do it again!" the cowboy said.

"If you insist," David said in his deep voice.

Nick closed the front door. He stood in the hallway. Overhead, the fluorescent light flickered. He dropped the duffel bag to the floor.

He touched the spike-studded, leather wristband, the one that helped him beat up that meathead the other night in Chicago. The wristband had been a gift from David on their five-year anniversary. Nick unstrapped it and dropped it on the floor.

The flickering fluorescent light blew out. Nick picked up his duffel bag and marched for the stairwell.

CHAPTER 14

Two days later, after dusk, Chase, Monique and Spanky hopped into the Astro Van. For a change, Chase drove.

Their destination was South Philly. Once there, Chase coasted down High Street. Three-quarters of the way down, Chase parked on the sidewalk. He had to. High Street was only wide enough for one car to drive down—the only place to park was on the sidewalk. Not that it mattered. This section of South Philly was more secluded that Jimmy Hoffa's eternal resting place.

Oddly, High Street wasn't so secluded twenty years ago. Back then, all kinds of trucks and cars traveled down it. The trucks docked and de-docked from the several factories lining the one side of the street; the cars arrived and departed from a diner at the end of the block. But that was decades ago. All the factories had closed down due to Philadelphia's astronomical business taxes, and the diner went out of business soon after. Nowadays, the only action High Street saw was on the weekends when hot rods raced down it as a shortcut to the nightclubs on Delaware Avenue.

Chase cut the Astro Van engine. He turned to Monique in the passenger seat.

"I'm going to stretch my legs," he said.

Monique nodded. In her lap was a sleeping Spanky.

Chase walked up the sidewalk he had parked the van on. He leaned against a brick wall and stared at the plant across the street. Barbed wire ran along the top of the chainlink fence. A sign on the gate noted that Mammon Bank owned the property.

A 747 roared overhead. Chase watched it and covered his ears, the plane's engines vibrating his bones. He had forgotten the Philadelphia International Airport was close by.

When the 747 disappeared from view, Chase saw Nick staggering up the street. Even though the sunset silhouetted him,

Noir Reunion

Chase knew it was Nick by his trademark gait. Only Nick's shoulders seesawed like that, although it did seem muted.

"What's up, punk?" Chase said, smiling.

"Hey."

Nick was carrying a duffel bag and his bass guitar. Chase noticed the circles around Nick's eyes, and his breath reeked as if he'd been using expired sour cream as toothpaste.

"Aw, man," Nick said, "I'm so fuckin' hungover."

"Is that why it looks like death warmed you over before rejecting you?"

Nick stared at the ground.

From the van, Monique waved and called Nick's name. He didn't respond. Just continued to stare down at the cracked sidewalk.

Chase tried catching Nick's attention by being comical. He quoted the old Nestle Crunch commercial: "Nicholas…Nicholas…"

Still nothing.

Monique slid out of the van with Spanky in tow. The sight of Spanky woke Nick out of his daze.

"What the fuck is that?" Nick asked.

"*This* is Spanky," Monique said. "Spanky, this is Nick. Say hi."

Spanky barked.

"Spanky's a harp seal," Monique explained.

"Man," Nick said, "what the fuck are you carrying a goddamned seal around for?"

Monique told the story of the hippie and the New Englander.

"So you swiped him after they were gone?" Nick said. "Wow, that's pretty punk rock."

"Watch this," Monique said, kneeling next to Spanky. "Spanky, show Nick what you think of California."

Spanky stuck his nose up in the air like a debutante.

"Now show him what you think of Philadelphia."

Spanky clapped his flippers together.

Nick grinned. Chase threw an arm around Nick's shoulder,

49

the bass getting in the way. "There we go," Chase said, "I knew we'd get a smile out of him eventually."

The three of them laughed for a couple moments. Nick was the first to stop. A frown overtook his face.

"What's wrong?" Monique asked.

"Nothing. I'm just hungover. That's all."

"Come on," Chase said. "What is it? You're more than hungover. We grew up together. We may not have hung out for a couple of years, but I know when something's bothering you. What's wrong?"

Nick hesitated. "I caught David with another guy."

"Your boyfriend?" Monique asked.

"Yeah, I came back from the tour a day early. Maybe it's a good thing I found out. I don't know. I guess I'm still in shock."

"You'll be fine," Monique said. "Just don't crawl into a bottle, okay?"

"Sure."

Spanky waddled up to Nick. The punk rocker squatted, then sat on the weed-covered curb to pet the seal. Spanky rested his head on Nick's lap and licked the punk rocker's palm.

"I'm still in love with him," Nick said, voice wavering. "Isn't that sick?"

"No," Monique said, "it's not." She joined him on the curb. "You'll feel that way for a long time. That's good. It means you're a better person than him."

Nick nibbled on his own lip.

"You'll find somebody else," Monique said. "I know it."

"I should've never moved in with him. I knew he had a history of infidelity when we first started dating, but I thought things would be different. You know?"

Chase squatted behind Nick and patted his back.

"I feel like such shit," Nick said. "And to top it all off, I'm homeless—not that I haven't been before, but it's different when your heart's been ripped out of your chest and stomped on by the person you thought was your soul mate."

"You'll be fine, bro," Chase said. "You'll be getting some

money coming your way. That should ease the pain a little."

"That's the only reason I showed up today: I need money. I've basically been sponging off David for the past five years. I get a little cash flow coming in from my music, but nowhere near enough to live on. Guess I should've started that record label I've always been wanting to do."

Chase couldn't squat on the sidewalk anymore. He rose with a groan and for circulation's sake strode to the middle of the street. Light from a utility pole shined down yellow, like a spotlight.

"Wait a minute," Chase said. "Are you telling me that you weren't going to show up today if everything was fine with David?"

"Uh, yeah," Nick said.

"What!"

Nick shrugged. "I didn't need the money. Now I do."

Chase was breathing hard. "But what about the pact we made twenty years ago to meet here today? That didn't mean anything to you?"

Nick shrugged again. Chase swore to himself if Nick shrugged one more time, he was going to run over and tear those shoulders out of their sockets.

"It's only money," Nick said. "I only need enough to live on. I don't care about being rich or putting money away for retirement. As long as I got my music, friends and a little love in my life, I'm cool."

"I don't believe this," Chase exclaimed. "You made a promise. I can't believe you were going to go back on your word!"

"Sorry," Nick said, playing with a hangnail.

"Calm down, hon," Monique said. "You can't expect people not to change over twenty years."

"Yeah, but—" Chase punched the air in an upward swing. He swung so hard that his jacket's zipper arched up and hit him in the neck. Felt like being hit with a pebble. "Getting this money means a lot to me. I don't want to be rich either, but I'm sick of the nine-to-five world. I hate being a wage-slave. If this score doesn't work out, then I'm going to be working shit jobs till the day I die."

"Hold on," Nick said, humor in his eyes. "Did you just say *score*?"

Chase blushed. "Yeah."

"What are you, Edward G. Robinson?"

"No," Chase said, fighting a smile.

In a Little Caesar voice, Nick said, "Now look here, see? We gotta score to settle, see? It's come down to this, Capone. Who's it gonna be? Me or the dame? You need to choose, see? Now I'm gonna count to ten. When I'm finished counting, I want a answer, and it better be the one I want to hear. Otherwise, it's curtains for you, and it ain't the kind they sell at Strawbridge's, see?"

Chase grinned so much, it hurt. "All right, all right. You got me. I'm through with being all melodramatic, okay?"

"Ah," Nick said, "I think I beat you out in the melodramatic department tonight, homey."

"Men," Monique said, rolling her eyes facetiously.

"Speaking of men," Chase said, glancing at his watch, "I wonder if Steve's gonna show. Not like he needs the money."

"True," Monique said.

CHAPTER 15

A thousand miles away, Steve Atkinson sat in his private plane. He looked out the window. Nothing to see below. Only cirrus clouds.

Steve closed his eyes for a second. *Let's see. We left Dallas at 1:30. That was what—an hour ago? Yes. So that means we're over Iowa now.*

Steve looked out the window again. He was glad the clouds blocked his view of Iowa. Who wanted to gaze down at that hick state, anyway?

A hand rested on Steve's leg. Red fingernails stroked his inner thigh.

"Keep going," Steve said.

The hand crept towards Steve's groin.

"You like that?" Buffy said.

Was that her name? No, Buffy was the TV show his daughter liked. Steve worried about the affect that *Buffy the Vampire Slayer* had on his daughter, Jessie. One night, while he was sleeping, would she drive a stake through his heart?

Okay. So Buffy wasn't the name of the bimbo who currently gave him a *dry job*. Hey, he just invented a word! Dry job: to play with a guy's pecker while he still wore his pants (variant of the term hand job). Steve should copyright *dry job* and market it to college students. Once *dry job* went into everyday usage, he would let online dictionaries include it in their databases, only after they paid licensing rights, of course.

All right, if Buffy wasn't this bimbo's name, then what was it? Steve remembered it started with a B. Bambi, Bonnie, Barbar…

"Hey, Bobbi," Steve said.

"Yes?" she whispered in his ear, her breath hot, smelling of rum.

"Do your thing."

Bobbi smiled. Steve saw each of her cuspids angled forty-

Johnny Ostentatious

five degrees towards her incisors. He hadn't noticed that when he picked her up in the airport bar, although, it was dark in there.

Bobbi bent over and unzipped Steve's pants. He tried to stay excited, but her L'Oreal hairdo kept stabbing his waist. Another turnoff were her flabs of fat. He hadn't noticed them before, but now they were glaringly apparent as she sprawled across the seat. She lay on her right side, the flabs visible on the left side of her black, velvety dress. (Bobbi had plenty of room to stretch out because the seat ran around the perimeter of the cabin in a U shape. There was a vestibule at the front of the plane for the cockpit, bathroom and entrance/exit door.)

Steve stared at the ceiling, concentrating on his erection. Bobbi's slurping helped, but after fifteen minutes he still hadn't ejaculated. He didn't understand. He usually came quicker than a teenager masturbating to Victoria's Secret.

Bored, Steve pulled out his cell phone from his briefcase. He called his wife.

"Hey," he said, "how are you? Uh-huh. I'm on my plane to Philadelphia. Huh?" Sigh. "I told *you*. I'm going out to meet some people I grew up with. That's right. The actor, the punk rocker and the actor's girlfriend—well, now wife. Hold on a second."

Steve put the phone on mute. He ejaculated. Bobbi tried jerking her head back. He snarled and dropped the phone. It bounced off her scalp, sounding similar to wood hitting cement. He clamped his hands on her head. Her hairspray stuck to his fingers like cotton candy.

"Swallow, you little whore. Swallow!"

Bobbi did as ordered, gulping audibly. Afterwards, she scrambled off the seat to the other side of the cabin, her eyes zipping back and forth.

Steve picked up the phone, taking it off mute. "Sorry about that. I had some urgent business to take care of." Pause. "Don't worry about it. I'd tell you, but it would wind up being over your head and confuse you more than you already are, you fucking dingbat. You know what, Victoria, I'm sick of talking to you.

Noir Reunion

Why? WHY? Because you're about as intellectually exciting as talking to that boob of an accountant I pay to keep my books clean. Do me a favor. Make yourself useful and put Jessie on."

Before his wife could retort the order, Steve put the phone back on mute.

Across the cabin, Bobbi sat on the seat, legs pulled into her chest, head on knees.

"You're a creep," she said so low, it was almost impossible to hear. Steve heard it because they were the words that had been screamed at him countless times before from downsized employees to jilted mistresses.

"I'm going to sue you for all you're worth," Bobbi said.

"Shut up, you skank," Steve said. "Make yourself useful and go read the sign by the cockpit."

Bobbi huffed to her feet. Arms crossed, she stalked to the cockpit area to read the sign that stated all persons boarding the plane agreed to forfeit all rights to file a lawsuit of any kind at any time against the Atkinson Corporation, its subsidiaries, or any of its employees.

Steve took the phone off mute. "Honey," he said, "you there?"

"*Hi, Daddy.*"

"How's my little girl?"

"*Okay. When you coming home?*"

"Probably not until next week. I'm heading out to Philadelphia on business."

"*Oh.*"

"How's your mother treating you?"

"*Okay. She's a little miffed 'cause I won't invite Becky Henderson to my birthday party on Saturday. She only wants me to invite her 'cause she's all buddy-buddy with Becky's mom.*"

"Becky Henderson... Which one's that again?"

"*She's got the freckles and really stringy hair and buck teeth.*"

"Bucktooth Becky?"

Steve's daughter giggled. "*Nobody calls her that anymore.*"

That's so fourth grade."

"Oh, that's right. You're in the fifth grade now. You're all grown up."

"*Dad!*"

"I guess pretty soon you won't have time to hang out with your old man. That is how you refer to me when with your friends, isn't it?"

"*No.*" His daughter tittered.

Steve watched Bobbi sulk from the cockpit area to her seat.

"Listen, kiddo," Steve said into the phone, "I have to go. Tell your mother I said you don't have to invite Bucktooth Becky if you don't want to."

"*'K.*"

"There's no reason why you should sacrifice your popularity because your mother is friends with Bucktooth Becky's mom. Understood?"

"*Mm-hmm.*"

"Good. I'll talk to you later."

"*Okay. Bye.*"

"Good-bye."

Steve disconnected. He had forgotten about Jessie's birthday. Why hadn't his assistant reminded him? He made a mental note to fire her, or at least deny her a cost-of-living raise at her next performance review. He also made a note to purchase an expensive present for Jessie. That should make up for missing her party.

Steve returned the cell to his briefcase and saw Bobbi, frowning, curl up in a ball on the seat and whimper.

Steve sneered.

CHAPTER 16

The Astro Van still sat on High Street. The darkness of the early evening was thick. Black clouds hovered over the abandoned factories, blocking any view of the smokestacks.

Monique paid no attention to the darkness. She led Spanky to the rear of the van. After opening the doors, she lifted the seal up and deposited him into the washtub. He frolicked in the ice like a blissful baby in a playpen. Monique closed the rear doors and headed around to the front passenger seat.

Chase sat in the driver seat. "I guess he isn't showing up." Steve.

"Can't say I'm surprised," Monique said. "He owns one of the biggest computer companies in the world. His share of the money is probably less than what he pays in taxes."

"You're probably right."

"Man," Nick said from the backseat, "I can't believe youse fuckin' brought a seal all the way from Cally. That's so goddamned hardcore."

"Thanks," Monique said, knowing Nick's comment was an observation, not a compliment.

"Come on," Chase said. "Let's get something to eat."

CHAPTER 17

At the end of High Street, Pierce Price sat in his Spyder. The Mitsubishi was in the parking lot of what used to be the High Street Diner. From this angle, Price had a clear view of Kilbey's Astro Van.

Price quit peering through his binoculars and mumbled, "Let's go, Kilbey. Where are you hiding the money?"

The Astro Van's engine turned over, rear taillights lighting up the deserted street in a red glow. Price started his Spyder and followed.

CHAPTER 18

Nick, Chase and Monique entered Come Anytime, a restaurant/bar in the Juanita borough of Philadelphia. Back in high school, Come Anytime was where everyone hung out. Mickey, the owner/bartender, served anyone sixteen years and older. If you were younger than that, you could stay, but Mickey wouldn't let you drink any alcoholic beverages. He had a sixth sense of a person's true age.

Nick had spent countless Friday nights here. One time, when he was fourteen, he made out in the utility closet with Lisa Herman, who was in the same grade as he. She was the class tomboy. Her black hair was short, she had beefy arms, and she was more aggressive than a football team on steroids. Not surprisingly, Lisa had made the first move on Nick, practically shoving him into the closet. Their petting session had been intense and sloppy. Nick still remembered how Lisa planted one hand on his lower back and clamped her other hand on the back of his head, as if she was afraid he would run away—no need to worry about that. After that night, they had dated for six months. In the twenty-two years since their courtship, Nick still thought about Lisa. He wondered if the basis of his attraction to her was accentuated masculinity. But no matter how often he wondered about it, he could never reach a conclusion. He would become distracted by the fact that nowadays Lisa was a hardcore, militant, parade-marching, man-hating lesbian. Go figure.

A waitress approached Nick, Chase and Monique. Her nametag read *Agnes*. Her white hair had a blue tinge and was pulled back into a bun. Two pens stuck out of the bun, giving her a geisha look—if there was such a thing as an eighty-year-old German geisha.

Nick, Chase and Monique followed Agnes to their table. Agnes limped; Nick and his friends didn't. She sat the trio in a secluded corner. Nick waited until Agnes was out of earshot before asking Chase and Monique, "Do you think the money'll still be there?"

"I don't see why not," Chase said.

"Maybe we should've scoped out the hiding spot a little closer."

"I don't—" Chase began but was interrupted.

"Well, looks like we're all here now," a voice said, its owner's shadow stretching across the table.

Nick, Chase and Monique looked up. There stood Steve Atkinson.

CHAPTER 19

Monique stared up at Steve. Even though she and Chase had seen Steve occasionally over the years, it still amazed her how much he had changed. As a teenager, he was the stereotypical nerd: face pussing with acne, athletic tape holding his glasses together, and enough grease in his hair to lube a U-joint. Now, he looked completely different. His hair was slicked back (thanks to coconut-smelling pomade), he no longer wore glasses and his power suit fit perfectly—probably tailor-made. The only characteristic that connected him to his high school days was his height. Five-five.

"Holy cow!" Chase said. "How are you, Steve?" Chase jumped up and hugged him. Monique noticed the computer tycoon stiffen.

"I'm good, I'm good," Steve answered. "Yourself?"

"All right, all right. Not bad..."

Chase and Steve sat down.

"How are you, Monique?" Steve asked.

"Good."

Steve took Monique's hand and shook it. Monique froze. Could Steve make the gesture any more flirtatious? Besides winking at her furtively, his middle finger grazed her palm. Monique's blood curdled. She yanked her hand away a little too quickly. Her elbow smacked her chair so hard, she winced. Chase and Nick didn't seem to notice.

"Hey, Mister Fashionably Late," Nick said, "what happened to your glasses?"

"Oh," Steve said, "I gave them up years ago. I was wearing contacts, but last year I underwent laser vision correction."

"You, hipster, you."

"I can't believe you're here," Chase said. "Didn't think you'd make it."

"As soon as I flew in, I instructed my driver to take me to

High Street, but I must have been too late, so I had him drive me here. I figured the three of you would be at the old hangout."

"Your powers of deduction are simply astounding," Nick said in a Ren Höek voice.

"Now we know why you're the multimillionaire," Chase said.

Steve smiled. Monique knew it was meant to be humble, but she recognized the smile for what it actually was. Conceitedness.

"So, how was your trip?" Steve asked Chase while looking at Monique.

"Not bad, not bad," Chase said. "It took us a week in our van. It's an interesting way to see the country. If you ever have a chance, do it."

"Yeah," Nick interjected, "but that shit can get old real quick. I've been on tour so many times, after awhile, towns and roads start to mesh into one another until it's one big cross-country, roadside blur."

Steve nodded with that conceited smile again. Monique wanted to reach across the table, grab him by his Christian Dior tie and shout in his face to act natural. He was with old friends, not business associates.

Agnes stopped by the table, asking if Steve wanted anything. He said no. A minute later, she brought out the food. Chase picked at his plate of spaghetti, while Nick attacked his meatloaf as if coming off a forty-days-and-forty-nights fast. *His hangover must be over*, Monique thought as she cut into her chicken teriyaki.

"So, Steve," Nick said, licking tomato sauce off the corner of his mouth, "not to be crass or anything, but how come you're here?"

"Out of loyalty," he said, as if rehearsed.

"That's cool, but the money we're going to get is pretty dirty. You sure you want to risk your upper-class status for your measly share of four million dollars?"

"Shhh!" Chase said.

Agnes limped towards them, leading a giggling group of

teenagers. She deposited them in the booth behind Nick.

Nick turned to the teenyboppers and said, "Hey kids, I don't mean to frighten youse or anything, but I had pork and beans for breakfast this morning, so if youse smell anything particularly rank, it'll be coming out of my anus."

The teenyboppers stared at one another, then broke out into guffaws. When they calmed down, Nick said, "Oh, by the way, see this guy here?" He pointed at Steve. "He's loaded, so eat and drink as much as you want. He's picking up the tab for the entire restaurant."

CHAPTER 20

Pierce Price listened to Nick Marsh's words: "...entire restaurant."

Price removed the earphone from his auricle. There was nothing else to hear.

Price sat in his Spyder parked across the street from Come Anytime. He recorded Kilbey and company's conversation with a microphone that doubled as the tip of the Spyder's antenna. The mike zeroed in on Kilbey's voice, blocking out all surrounding sounds except other voices within ten feet. The conversation was recorded into a laptop, in a WAV file. Price tapped the touch pad of his laptop, saved the file, then put the computer in hibernation mode and tucked it under the passenger seat.

It started to rain. Price touched a button on the rear door. The window rolled up with a whir.

For fifteen minutes, the precipitation alternated between a drizzle and a light rain. Then the rain fell in copious amounts. Not enough to discourage you from running an errand, but you'd definitely need an umbrella or poncho.

Price watched raindrops land on the Spyder hood. The drops raced down the car to the hood ornament.

A knock on the window broke the hypnotic effect the rain held over Price. Through the fogged-up window, he saw hairy knuckles rap the window again. He rolled down the window. *Whirrrrr.* Rain landed on Price's lap. He shivered slightly.

"What?" Price said.

"Out." Hairy Knuckles pointed a thumb.

"But it's my car."

"Don't give me a hard time, Price."

"But..." Price sighed, then got out of the car, stomped around to the other side and huffed into the passenger seat, slamming the door behind him. He crossed his arms and pouted.

Noir Reunion

Hairy Knuckles lounged behind the steering wheel as if he had been sitting there for hours, not seconds. He rolled down the window to let his arm hang outside, cigar and all. Hairy Knuckles' birth name was Bruno Savage.

Price stared at Savage. God, how he hated him. Price hated everything about him. He hated the beige trench coat that Savage always wore. He hated Savage's balding head and the endless dandruff it produced. He hated Savage's ubiquitous facial stubble. He hated Savage's bowling-ball-size belly. But most of all, he hated how Savage subjected him to servant status. Price was accustomed to giving orders, not receiving them. It was a role he could do without. He relished being the boss, not the whipping boy.

"Something on your mind?" Savage asked, eyes on Come Anytime.

"No," Price said.

"Then quit looking at me like that." Savage made eye contact. "Capeesh?"

Saying nothing, Price looked away. Savage's eyes scared him. They were constantly bloodshot, and more sclera showed than iris and pupil. Plus, Savage's eyelids drooped more than a stoner's, but the odd thing was that he was intellectually sharp and quick with the gun.

Price held his breath. He wished Savage would roll up the window. The door, the dash and the steering wheel were getting soaked. Price bit the inside of his cheek. Didn't it bother Savage that his pants were getting wet?

"Any news?" Savage asked.

"Nothing worthwhile." Price recapped what Kilbey and his friends had discussed.

Savage took a drag from his cigar. He exhaled towards the windshield. Most of the smoke wafted in Price's direction. He coughed. He couldn't wait until they found out where Kilbey and his friends had stashed the cash. Price would take his half and speed away in his Spyder, never to see Savage again. *Sayonara, shithead!*

Johnny Ostentatious

Price cleared his throat. "So...have you thought about how you're going to spend your two million?"

Savage didn't answer.

"First," Price said, "I'm going to take a trip to Europe. I've always wanted to get my willy wet in Paris. When I get back, I'm going to invest in some real estate, maybe something down in Florida. What about you? Are you going to invest any of it?"

Almost imperceptibly, Savage shrugged. "Haven't given it much thought."

"What!"

"I've been more focused on *getting* the money than fantasizing how I'm going to spend it. It's a practical way to approach the situation. Something you should look into."

"Yeah, but two million dollars each. Two. Million. Dollars. Doesn't that excite you even a little?"

"Not really. It's not in my possession yet. More than anything else, I'm more concerned with getting even with those kids."

Price gulped. "Are you going to kill them?"

"Haven't decided yet. Depends on how things play out. If they put up a fight, sure, I may have to kill one or two of them. If they don't put up a fight, I'll let 'em walk. They won't go to the police. They're in far too deep."

Price nodded. Rain pitter-pattered on the Spyder roof. He wondered if it rained this time of the year in Paris.

CHAPTER 21

Chase and Monique stood in the vestibule of Come Anytime. Nick and Steve were still inside. The Kilbeys stood next to the vestibule's cigarette machine. Outside, rain shot down from the sky in a slant. The rhythm of the slant was disrupted occasionally by a mild wind.

Chase stood behind Monique. He wrapped his arms around her and kissed her neck. One of her hands rose. She stroked his cheek.

Nick and Steve entered the vestibule from the restaurant.

"Oh, for crying out loud!" Nick said, beaming. "Get a room, you two!"

"Why," Chase said, "you want to watch?"

"Like I ain't got shit better to do than watch you two lame-ass heteros bump and grind like two extras in a rap video."

"Nick," Steve said, "what was that?"

"What? Did that stud at the bar flirt with me? Did I miss it?"

"No, announcing to the entire restaurant that I would pick up the tab."

"What," Nick said, smirking, "are your credit cards all maxed out?"

"No, but that was completely inappropriate."

"Why, you got something against spreading the wealth?"

Steve, as if to calm himself, glanced down at his cupped hands. "That's not the point. You didn't consult me before making the announcement."

"Why, would've you said no?"

Steve didn't answer.

Chase stopped hugging Monique. He didn't like where this was going.

"So tell me, *Mister* Atkinson," Nick said, "if I would've 'consulted' you, would you still pick up the tab?"

"That's not the point," Steve said.

"What is the point, Poindexter?"

Steve stood in the middle of the vestibule, hands on hips, suit coat open, his pressed white dress shirt practically glaring. "The point is I work hard for my money. I didn't get to where I am today in order to give it away to people who didn't earn it."

Chase saw Nick's right eye twitch. He knew what that meant. Nick was about to get medieval on Steve's ass. Chase didn't like that. He hated to see friction or confrontation among people, especially friends.

A nuclear family of four entered the vestibule from outside. The husband, wife and two children of junior-high age (the boy older than his sister) walked past Chase and Monique, then between Nick and Steve. Good thing too, Chase thought. The family's brief appearance diffused Nick and Steve's argument. Neither seemed intent on continuing it—at least not now.

The nuclear family went into the restaurant, the wood door with mosaic glass clicking behind them.

Monique said, "We should get going."

CHAPTER 22

Bruno Savage perked to attention. Chase Kilbey and his fellow perps exited Come Anytime. The one perp, Steve Atkinson, spoke curtly to a limousine driver. The limo drove away. Atkinson joined the other three perps at the Astro Van.

Savage kept his eyes on the van. Price said something, but Savage ignored him. Ninety percent of what came out of Price's mouth was inconsequential.

The Astro Van pulled out of its parking spot. Savage started the Spyder and followed, a purple Dodge Neon between them.

Price said, "Shouldn't we be at least three cars back from them?"

"Shut up," Savage said.

It had stopped raining. Nonetheless, traffic moved slower than a tortoise race. Savage yawned. He fought boredom by picturing a scenario of the perps retrieving the four million dollars.

The perps would hug the money while jumping up and down, ecstatic over their long-anticipated wealth. That's when Savage and Price would barge in, take the money and shoot the perps. Savage had lied to Price about that. For a long time, Savage had planned on killing Chase Kilbey and his partners in crime. Savage would order the four perps to lay on the ground, then shoot them in the following order: Atkinson, Marsh, Flemming, Kilbey. Savage wanted Kilbey to die last so he could see his friends and his wife die before he received a bullet in the back of the head.

Another lie Savage had told Price was that he didn't care about the money. Of course he cared about the money. Why else had he spent the last five years tracking Kilbey down?

Up until 1998, Savage had been a detective for the Philadelphia Police. The department fired him after a lengthy Internal Affairs Division investigation. The IAD case was so strong,

Johnny Ostentatious

Savage lost his appeals quicker than you could say Thomas Jones. Savage even failed to get the IAD ruling reversed at arbitration—unheard of in a corrupt city like Philly.

Part of Savage's termination included the forfeiting of his pension. So, at the age of fifty-four, Savage became a daily reader of the classifieds. The best job he could get was a night-shift watchman at a retirement home.

In his spare time, Savage worked on finding Kilbey, which took awhile. It wasn't until last year that he discovered Kilbey's whereabouts. That's when Savage contacted Price. Fortunately, Price was greedy enough to be Savage's eyes on the West Coast.

"They're turning, they're turning!" Price said.

"Keep your panties on," Savage said.

The Astro Van turned down High Street.

"Aren't you going to follow them?" Price asked.

Savage shook his head. "If we follow them, they'll know they're being tailed."

"Oh."

Savage made a U-turn, switched off the Spyder's headlights and parked in what was once the High Street Diner parking lot. He cut the engine and asked Price, "When you were tailing them earlier, did they spot you?"

"No," Price said, "I parked here, actually."

"Then why did you ask me if I was going to follow them?"

"I didn't realize where we were at first," Price said, popping the glovebox. He rummaged around, receipts falling to the floor, eventually pulling out a pair of miniature binoculars.

Savage swiped them.

"Hey!" Price said.

"Shut up. Make yourself useful and take a nap."

Savage aimed the binoculars at the windshield. He couldn't see anything. It may have stopped raining but visibility was poor. High Street had only one utility pole light and Kilbey had parked past it. It didn't help that a fog was settling in.

"Here." Savage tossed the binoculars on Price's lap. Price swooped them up and squinted through them, the wrong way at

first.
 Savage massaged his stubbly chin. He was looking forward to the confrontation with the four perps. After shooting them, he was going to kill Price. And who knew, if things went awry, Savage just might off himself, too.

CHAPTER 23

Steve sat in the van on the seat that lined the passenger-side wall. He looked at the harp seal in the washtub full of ice. The seal barked angrily at him. Steve didn't flinch. What he wouldn't give to club the seal to a pulpy death. That would be...satisfying.

Monique slid out of the passenger seat and knelt next to the seal. "What's wrong, Spanky?"

The seal continued to bark at Steve. He tried to appear innocent, but Monique was obviously not buying it. She petted the seal's head while holding Steve's gaze.

Steve didn't mind staring at Monique. She was so beautiful, he could ogle her all day and not get bored. Of course, he'd prefer to ogle her as she was pinned under him, which would become a reality by the end of his stay here in Philadelphia. He would seduce her, and she'd love every minute of it. How could she resist? He was one of the richest people in the world. And as history has proven time and time again, the rich *always* get what they want.

"We're here," Chase said from the driver's seat.

Steve, Chase, Nick and Monique piled out of the van. They stood in the street. A decrepit plant loomed down at them. It was six stories. Half of its oversized windows were missing or cracked; the other half were graffitied on. A sign on the roof said *Taylor Manufacturing*.

"Are you sure the money is still in there?" Steve asked.

"Not one hundred-percent sure," Chase said, "but we stuck it in a good spot. There's no reason why it shouldn't be there. Even if they demolished the place and built something else, we'd probably still be able to get to the money. You know?"

"Hey," Nick exclaimed, "check out the size of that puddle."

He skipped up the street to the puddle in question. It was a foot long, covered the curb, and was four feet in diameter. Nick jumped in the puddle, brown rainwater splashing. A drop of water reached the cuffs of Steve's Versace pants. Sighing, he stepped back.

"Come on, people," Nick said, "regress with me! It'll be fun."

Monique hopped over. She took Nick's hand, and they splashed around like two kids let out of school early. Steve wanted to jog over and hold Monique's other hand, but he didn't want to ruin his suit.

Eventually, Nick and Monique quit jumping around. Monique joined a grinning Chase standing by the van.

"Man," Nick said, "that was fun. Hey, listen to this."

He stamped his feet down. His Chuck Taylor high-tops squished and left logo imprints on the dry sidewalk.

Steve rolled his eyes. *Faggot.*

"You hear that?" Nick said. "I think I got a little, itty-bitty goldfish swimming around in there."

Steve pinched the bridge of his nose. He needed to gain control of the situation. If he didn't, Nick would continue with his Adam Sandler act.

"Did your dad work here until the company closed down?" Steve asked Chase.

Chase didn't answer right away. He was staring at the plant. Finally, he said, "They actually 'let him go' a year before he could retire, so he had to go out looking for work at the youthful age of fifty-nine. He couldn't find a job that paid as well as Taylor, so he wound up working a bunch of odd jobs for six years."

"Six years!" Nick said, no longer jovial.

"Yeah," Chase said. "He had to work that long to keep paying the health insurance for him and my mom."

"That sucks."

Chase nodded. "It was a total blow to his self-esteem. He started working at Taylor the day after high school. I think he took being fired personally. But the odd jobs sort of worked out for him. At first, he was working something like eighty hours a week, then, with each passing year, he was working less and less.

So he kind of eased into retirement."

"That's cool," Nick said.

"Being downsized was always a sore spot with him," Chase said. "You couldn't even joke about it when he was around. If you did, he'd mope around for the rest of the day."

"Shit," Nick said.

Chase's head motioned towards the plant. "He really loved being a foreman here."

"Fuckin' corporations."

Steve cleared his throat. He couldn't keep quiet anymore. He had to educate these peasants. "Can I say something?"

"You just did," Nick quipped.

"When a company hires you," Steve said, "they're only renting your time for forty hours a week. There's no reason why your whole identity should become part of your job."

"Pardon my German," Nick said, "but that's the biggest fuckin' load of horse shit I heard since George W's State of the Union Address. What about when a company makes you work overtime?"

"That's needed occasionally in order to maintain profitability and productivity. Besides, employees are compensated for their time."

"What?" Nick snickered. "What kind of airplane glue are you huffing?"

"Excuse me?"

"Profit? Productivity? What kind of crap is that?"

"That's...reality."

"Reality! What, so you can get rich off the labor of the underprivileged?"

Steve shrugged. "That's the way the world works."

Nick made a sound like a game-show buzzer. "Wrong again, el nerdo. That's not how the world works. That's how this stupid society works: the top one percent of the population exploiting the toils of the poor."

"You still don't get it, do you?"

"I get that our society needs a major overhaul."

Noir Reunion

"And what do you suggest be done to correct the system?"

"First off," Nick said, "get rid of capitalism. That's a major part of the problem."

"Isn't that the same song and dance you were singing back in high school?"

"Don't fix what ain't broke. Know what I'm sayin', *Mister Millionaire*?"

Steve leaned forward. "So tell me this, Nick, what are you doing to change things? Is playing in a punk-rock band going to change the world?" Steve watched Nick's tongue peek between his lips. Steve suppressed a smirk. Nick was scrambling for a comeback. Endorphins pumped through Steve's brains. *Atkinson 1, Marsh 0.*

"Tell me this," Steve said. "Do you really think when people hear your music, they're influenced to 'make a difference.' No, they're not. You know why? Because you're preaching to the converted. You're not winning over anybody."

"Bullshit," Nick said, a croak in his voice.

"Are you sure?"

Nick turned away.

Steve, grinning, said, "You're an entertainer, Nick. Deal with it."

"There's nothing wrong with that," Monique said.

Chase appeared thoughtful. Steve knew Chase was mulling over whether to take his or Monique's side. He would probably take his wife's, since he was pussywhipped—like most *happily* married men. But before Chase could decide whose side to take, Steve needed to insult Nick one last time.

"True," Steve said, meeting Monique's vehement pupils, "there's nothing dishonorable about being an entertainer, but you have to admit, most entertainers take more than they give. They steal the audience's attention and money, while the audience gets nothing more than a slight distraction for a couple hours—and a lighter wallet. It's a pretty unfair exchange, if you ask me."

"Nobody was asking you," Monique said.

Steve nodded. Peripherally, he saw Nick's cheeks shade purple. That pleased Steve more than a stock split.

A 767 flew overhead, marking an end to the bickering.

"So," Steve said pleasantly, "are we doing this tonight?" His chin pointed towards the plant.

"I don't know," Chase said, turning to Monique, "what do you think?"

"I think we should do it during the day," she said. "It's dark in there—we're going to need as much light as possible."

Cheeks still purple, Nick said, "We should do it early, around dawn. I know this street doesn't draw a lot of traffic, but we should play it safe. I doubt if any cops'll wanna cruise down here at six o'clock in the morning."

"Good point," Monique said.

"We'll also need flashlights."

Nick's voice cracked on the word flashlights. *Good,* Steve thought, *he's still shook up by my comments. I'm the one in control.*

"Right," Chase said. "Flashlights. I forgot all about them."

"It's supposed to rain tonight into tomorrow," Monique announced. "Maybe we should do it the day after."

Chase and Steve nodded.

"Smells like a plan," Nick said.

1983

CHAPTER 24

In a popular culture sense, the early 1980s were a fertile time. John Hughes movies promoted teenage flicks from flash-trash to flawless works of art. New Wave permeated the airwaves with the second British Invasion, i.e., Culture Club, Duran Duran and The Police. And Stephen King was in his prime with books like *Christine, Different Seasons* and *Pet Sematary*.

Nineteen eighty-three was a particularly notable year. It was when the decade began to find its identity. There was still some residue from the disco-laden seventies, but times were good, especially since it was seven years away from when the media arrogantly and inappropriately labeled the era the "Me Decade."

Chase thought about none of this, of course. He was too worried about idling his Camaro in the middle of McKinley Street.

McKinley was a one-way side street that had a high accident rate because cars sped off an adjacent highway, the twelve-lane Roosevelt Boulevard, at a minimum of thirty miles per hour. There was no place to parallel park on McKinley during the day since most of the street's residents worked the night shift and slept while the sun was up—their cars and trucks taking up all of the available parking spots.

Chase continued to idle near the Boulevard turn-off. He glanced in his rearview mirror. It vibrated thanks to the Camaro's V-6 engine.

"Come on, Nick," Chase muttered, honking his horn.

Every day, for the past month (since getting his license), Chase had driven his best friend, Nick, to school. And every day, Nick was late. Even when Chase was delayed, showing up five to ten minutes past 7:30 A.M., Nick still wasn't on time.

Finally, Nick moseyed out of his mom's house, backpack in hand.

"Come on," Chase said, "let's go!"

"What's the rush?" Nick asked. "We got plenty of time.

School don't start f—"

Even though Nick had only one foot in the Camaro, Chase hit the gas.

"Whoa!" Nick pulled his dragging foot in and slammed shut the door. "What the fuck, man?"

Chase pointed at the rearview mirror. A Mustang had screeched off Roosevelt Boulevard at fifty miles per hour. The driver of the Mustang hit the brakes, missing the Camaro's bumper by a piston ring.

"Shit," Nick said in a low voice.

"You really need to start being on time." Chase coasted his Camaro through a stop-sign intersection.

"Ah, we're fine, as long as you got that sixth sense of when cars are coming."

"You're messed up, dude."

Nick snarled like Billy Idol and said, "In the midnight hour…with a rebel yell."

Chase laughed.

CHAPTER 25

Nick's Spanish class let out early. He darted out of the room quicker than you could say *buonas diaz, senior* and skipped down the marble steps to the cafeteria.

The caf hit Nick with its usual stench, a mixture of ammonia and cooking oil. The caf looked as it did every other day. Yellow floor tiling, limestone walls and white drop ceiling.

Nick was the first student to arrive for lunch. He aimed for his usual table in the back, by the vending machines. To the left of the vending machines was the janitor, Mr. Solinski, who repaired a leaking trashcan with paper towels.

Nick dropped his books on the table. The table groaned. Nick opened his beaten brown paper bag and removed his lunch: a peanut-butter-and-jelly sandwich. While eating his PB-n-J, Nick read the latest issue of *Maximumrocknroll*. The punk-rock zine had interviews with his two favorite bands, The Circle Jerks and The Angry Samoans. Halfway through The Circle Jerks Q&A, Nick caught sight of Chase sauntering up the aisle. Chase plunked his books on the table. Nick's Hawaiian Punch splashed around in its bottle.

"Z'up?" Nick said.

"G'day, governor," Chase said in a Cockney accent.

Nick smiled. Every day at lunch, Chase greeted people with a different accent. He never failed to entertain.

"What's going on?" Chase asked.

"Same shit, different life," Nick replied through a mouth half full of Skippy and Smuckers.

"Hey, I hear ya, sister."

Chase opened a pack of Gummi Bears with his teeth. He popped a yellow one in his mouth, swished it around, spit it out, then tossed it heavenward. It stuck to the ceiling, along with the other Gummi Bears and pencils that students had flung up there since September. Every summer, Mr. Solinski extracted enough

Johnny Ostentatious

pencils and Gummi Bears from the caf ceiling to fill a tree trunk. Steve approached the table. "Hi," he said, not making eye contact. Nick and Chase returned the greeting.

Nick and Chase were sitting across from each other at the end of the table. Steve sat one chair away from Chase and plopped his skyscraper stack of textbooks on the table. *What does he do*, Nick thought, *carry every one of his books around with him all day?*

Steve hunched over, nibbling on what his alcoholic mother packed for him every day. Tuna fish.

Dandruff and eyebrow grease dirtied the lenses of Steve's Coke-bottle eyeglasses. A pang of pity rose up in Nick for a moment. He noticed that one of the nose pads on Steve's glasses was missing—must've lost it. In its place was a wad of cotton ball. Nick looked away. Christ, how poor was Steve's family, anyway?

Nick stopped thinking about Steve's economic situation. The caf was filling up. As more students piled in, the decibel level rose, courtesy of girls gossiping and jocks grunting.

Nick spoke over the noise to tell Chase about the used bass guitar he bought over the weekend. Halfway through the recount, Nick realized Chase wasn't listening. He was staring across the caf. Nick decided to have some fun with Chase's inattention.

"So, anyway," Nick said, "I'm at the counter, and I ask the salesman how much the bass is. He says, 'Well, we have a couple different pricing policies. If you're only gonna buy the bass, it's two hundred, but if you want the bass and a tattoo, too, it's one fifty.' So I'm like, 'A tattoo? That's not a bad idea. What kind you got?' He says, 'Well, we have a bunch of different kinds. But I think the one that would fit your personality is this one.' He shows me one that says MIRACLE GROW. So I ask him what that's all about. 'Oh,' he says, 'we stick it on your dick.' 'Really?' I say. 'Or we have this one,' he says and shows me another one I can stick on my dick. It says THIS END UP."

"Uh-huh," Chase said, sliding out of his chair. "I'll be back."

Nick turned to Steve. "Do you think it was something I

said?"

Steve didn't reply. He continued nibbling on his tuna fish sandwiched between two slices of Stroehmann King bread. A glob of mayonnaise hung from the corner of his mouth.

Nick watched Chase stride across the caf. Chase stopped at every other table to say hi to classmates. Nick always found it remarkable that Chase, a social chameleon, could fit in with almost every clique in school, while Nick and Steve, outcasts of their class, could only relate to those who shared their interests (punk rockers in Nick's case, computer programmers in Steve's). Nick thought Chase's willingness to hang out with him and Steve was pretty decent. After all, Chase could've hung out with one of the popular crowds instead of with the school's two biggest misfits. Nick sometimes wondered why Chase considered Steve and him his two best friends, but he never asked. Probably had something to do with the three of them being seated together in the same kindergarten class.

Nick lost sight of Chase. The lunch crowd was thickening. Some of the students moved for the courtyard. The door to the courtyard was next to the vending machine, where Nick sat. Cigarette smoke wafted in. Nick coughed. God, how he hated cigarettes. Besides being a slow form of suicide, cigarette smoking made greedy tobacco companies richer. Nick's mom puffed on two packs of Salems a day.

Chase returned to the table, grinning like a lottery winner.

"What are you beaming about?" Nick asked.

"Got a date for the prom."

"Really? Who with?"

"Monique Flemming," Chase said proudly.

"Monique Flemming?" Nick squinted across the caf. "Who the hell's that?"

"A transfer from Cardinal Dougherty," Steve interjected.

"How do you know that?"

"She's in two of my classes, biology and Shakespeare."

"Ooooo," Nick said, "a little Romeo-and-Juliet action. Hop to it, Chase! Just steer clear of the hemlock."

Johnny Ostentatious

"She's so hot, Nick. Wait till you see her."

Nick nodded, worried that he didn't have a date for the prom yet.

CHAPTER 26

Steve sat behind his desk in biology class. The teacher, Ms. Krentz, drew a diagram on the blackboard. Any other day, Steve would be drooling at the sight of Ms. Krentz's backside, her skirt rising as she reached to the top of the blackboard to finish drawing the diagram. But today Ms. Krentz aroused him about as much as Mother Theresa, even though Ms. Krentz wore a tight blue dress, which accentuated her cleavage and freckled chest.

Why no interest in Ms. Krentz today? One simple reason. Monique Flemming, the transfer student.

Monique sat in the aisle to Steve's right. She was two seats up, so Steve had an excellent view of her legs. Her plaid skirt barely reached her knees, and she wore black shoes over lacy ankle-high, white socks. Her legs were crossed. The leg on top rocked back and forth, hypnotizing him, like a metronome. Every few minutes she switched legs, a dimple forming for a moment on the side of the knee of her bottom leg. Currently, the left leg was over the right. Steve wanted so badly to go over there and caress those luscious legs. God, how he loved legs.

Steve tried to stop staring at Monique's legs and concentrate on Ms. Krentz's lesson, but it was about as easy as solving the traveling salesman problem. Steve finally managed to focus on the day's lesson, but first made a mental note to fantasize about Monique after school today when he masturbated in his bathroom. Usually, he imagined Ms. Krentz str—

"Mr. Atkinson."

Steve sat up straight. His heartbeat vibrated through his body.

"Mr. Atkinson," Ms. Krentz said again. "Please come up and show us where the stamen is."

"The stamen?" Steve managed to croak.

"Yes, on the flower I've drawn on the blackboard."

"It's in the center of the flower, near the pedals," Steve said.

Ms. Krentz motioned for Steve to step in front of the class.

Johnny Ostentatious

He remained frozen in his seat. He couldn't go up there. Not now.

"Mr. Atkinson, I'd hate to see your A-plus average plummet due to an unsatisfactory mark in participation."

"I can't," Steve mumbled, Adam's apple bobbing, not sure if Ms. Krentz heard him. He said it so low that Ricky Fendora, the class clown, who sat in front of him, probably didn't hear it.

"Mr. Atkinson," Ms. Krentz said, "do not try my patience today." She placed a manicured hand on one of her supermodel-shaped hips. "I'm going to count to three, and if you're not up here, I'm going to be *very* disappointed. "One..." Why was she doing this to him? "...two..." He was the best student in the class. She never humiliated him. Maybe she'd caught him drooling over Monique's legs and was jealous. "...three."

Steve stood up. His erection throbbed. He walked up the aisle. The class, except for Monique, started laughing. Steve's cheeks flushed purple. His erection wouldn't abate. It was starting to ache. Maybe thinking about ice would weaken it. Nope. It was still hard as a Lotus textbook. Maybe thinking about computer codes would make it go away. No, bad idea. Anything computer related got him excited. How about English? That was a boring subject. He could mentally recite that ho-hum poem he had to study last night. Who was it by again? That's right, Anne Sexton.

"Quiet, class," Ms. Krentz said. The laughing subsided. "Mr. Atkinson."

Steve's eyes met Ms. Krentz's. For a second, he thought he read a secret message in those blue irises: *Stevie, honey, get through this and I'll thank you after school...in the bedroom of my apartment.*

"Mr. Atkinson," Ms. Krentz said in the authoritarian voice of a veteran librarian.

"Yes?"

"The stamen, Mr. Atkinson." Ms. Krentz nodded at the blackboard. "Where is it?"

Steve gaped. She was still going to make him go through

Noir Reunion

with it!

"The stamen, Mr. Atkinson," she repeated. "Where is it?"

"In his pants," Ricky Fendora said.

The class broke out in hysterics. Ms. Krentz gave a detention-dispensing glare, which silenced everyone except Monique. She didn't need admonishing because she hadn't displayed one expression of enjoyment since this episode began. For that, Steve was grateful.

Blocking out Monique and the rest of the class, Steve picked up the chalk. He looked down at his penis. Jeez, was it getting bigger? For how embarrassed he was, he thought it would have went at least a little flaccid.

With the chalk in his left hand, Steve circled the stamen. Simultaneously, he placed his right palm flat against the blackboard, where nothing was written.

"Thank you, Steven," Ms. Krentz said, not making eye contact. "You may return to your seat."

Steve dropped the chalk; his palm left a sweaty imprint on the blackboard. He rushed back towards his seat. A few classmates sneered. When he reached his seat, his boner disappeared like a fourteen-minute celebrity.

Sweat dripped off Steve's brow. He was shaking, too. But he kept his eyes on his desk. In his notebook, somebody has written LOSER! in red ink and underlined it six times (the third underline had torn through the page). Steve ripped the page out. On the next page, someone else had written NERD. It looked as if it had been written quickly. Steve crumbled up both sheets of paper and dropped them to the floor.

They'll all be sorry one day. I'll show them who the loser is.

Steve looked over at Monique. She turned. Her lips mouthed the word sorry. He tried to show gratitude by smiling but instead grimaced. She turned around slowly.

Steve stared down at his notebook. The impression from the two torn-out pages shouted at him:

NERD

LOSER!

Johnny Ostentatious

Steve closed the notebook and fought back tears. *One day I'm going to show them all.*

CHAPTER 27

7 P.M., Saturday night.
Monique sat at the mirror in her bedroom, crimping one last lock of hair, then tucking it behind her ear. Smiling at her do, she unplugged her iron. The cord lay across a book she'd been reading for leisure. *The Grifters* by Jim Thompson.
Monique stood up and walked across the bedroom to the window. She hit the stop button of her Sony cassette player. The soundtrack to *Valley Girl* stopped playing; New Wave notes echoed. Monique turned on the radio. The Go-Go's bragged how they got the beat.
Monique stepped in front of her body-length mirror. She slipped into her shoes and gave one last appraisal of her blue, satiny dress. *Looking good*, she thought.
Opening her bedroom door, her shadow passing over her "Save The Seals" poster, Monique heard her father's cigar-tinged voice talking to Chase in the living room:
"So me and my buddies are walking down the street on the way to the Eagles game, when all of the sudden, this guy in a real fancy suit and slicked-back hair walks up to us. He's carrying a suitcase the size of Veteran's Stadium and is wearing a smile that reminds me of those PBS documentaries. You know the ones. The Jacques Cousteau ones, where he's underwater in a cage to go white-shark watching. You know when the sharks go by, and you can see all their teeth—like they're smiling. That's what this guy looked like. Anyways, he steps in front of us. My pal Richie says, 'Can I help you?' And this guy says, 'Good afternoon, gentlemen. I was wondering if you could give me a couple minutes of your time?' 'Listen,' I tell him, 'we're kinda in a rush. The game's about to start.' 'This'll only take a minute,' he says, then opens his humongous suitcase and pulls out a stand, the kind waiters use in big fancy restaurants to set down their trays. Me and my buddies can't see what's in the suitcase 'cause

Johnny Ostentatious

this guy's got it sitting on the stand, turned away from us. Needless to say, our interest is piqued. My pal Richie says, 'What're ya selling there, Jack?' The guy pretends not to hear and says, 'Gentlemen, you look like a bunch of hard-working joes. Like Donna Summer says, I bet you work hard for your money. You don't like spending any more than you have to. Am I right, or am I right?' My buddies, Richie included, start nodding their heads, but I'm not. As a kid, I spent a couple summers working for the SPCA, so I can smell shit a couple counties away. And this guy reeks like a kennel that hasn't been cleaned in weeks. 'Gentlemen,' the guy says, 'I won't keep you long. I don't want you to miss any of the big game. Real quick, let me ask you this. What hurts more than a quarterback sack?' 'Gettin' a root canal,' my pal Charlie says. 'Seeing my ex-wife,' I say sarcastically. 'Paying my kids' tuition,' Richie says. Suddenly, the guy—this salesman—his eyes light up. Richie gave him the opening he was looking for. 'Paying school tuition is tough,' he tells us. 'I should know. I'm putting six kids through school. Paying that tuition means you have less money for who? That's right. You. Your kids are receiving a free ride at your expense. That means there's less money in the bank account for what *you* would like to buy. I can't help but notice that none of you are sporting any Eagles paraphernalia. Could it be because Eagles merchandise is too expensive?' Before I could unzip my jacket and show him by Jaworski jersey, he turns the suitcase around so we can finally see what's inside. And you know what it is? Guess. Give up? Counterfeit Eagles stuff. Jerseys, sweats, action figures. You name it, this jerky was hawking it. Looking at it, I saw why he went through that epic spiel of his. Right off the bat, you could tell this stuff was fake. The white lettering on the Eagles jersey bleeded into the green. Same with the sweats. And the action figures were obviously *Star Wars* action figures repainted to look like starters—they all looked like Hanz Solo, or whatever the hell his name is. Then comes the kicker. Richie asks, 'Hey, how much for the—' But I cut him off before he can finish. I say to the salesman, 'You scum-bucket!' Then I dive for him, knocking his suitcase full of junk over into Passyunk Avenue. The salesman starts screaming like a prissy little schoolgirl. He tries running away, but I catch him by the back of the neck. My hand slips at first 'cause of the goo he's got in his hair, but I then get a nice hold on him. I take this little twerp and throw him into the parking lot's chainlink fence. I throw him so hard, the entire fence does this wave all the way down the block. The twerp bounces off the fence. I force him to turn around. His lower lip's quivering like he's freezing to death. I slam him against the fence. His back hits one of the posts, so the whole fence doesn't shake this time. I grab him by his lapels and press my nose against his. His breath reeks of peppermints. I then begin shouting at him, taking out all my frustrations over all the sleazy salesmen me and my family and friends have ever been manipulated by. You know?"

"Dad," Monique said, walking down the stairs, "are you telling that silly story again?"

"Hey," her father said, "that story improves with age."

"Oh, please."

"Anyway, Chase," Mr. Flemming said, "I slapped that salesman around some. Roughed him up a little—nothing major. Just enough to put a little scare in him, you know, so maybe he might think about another line of work. Then me and my buddies went off to the game."

Monique reached the landing. Her father took her hand. His callused palms didn't bother her. She actually liked them. It was a sign of masculinity.

"You look great," Chase and Mr. Flemming said in unison.

"Thanks," Monique said, blushing.

Monique couldn't believe how sexy Chase looked in his tux. His blue tie complemented his cobalt eyes, and mousse gave his hair a spiky effect. Monique winked; Chase grinned.

After Chase pinned a white corsage on Monique, relatives and neighbors poured in for the next half-hour. They took so many pictures that Monique saw red dots every time she blinked.

One of the neighbors, Mrs. Fletcher, brought her German

shepherd, Chomper, to the *photo session*. Chomper had the temperament of an unrepentant sociopath. He was infamous in the neighborhood for scaling ten-foot-high fences in a single bound, all to pounce on postal carriers. Chomper was the reason why Philadelphia Post Office supervisors let carriers in this section of Northeast Philly pack tranquilizer guns.

Chomper wasn't in the Flemming home for five seconds when he started barking like a Cujo clone. Mrs. Fletcher yanked the leash, but all that did was make Chomper stand on his hind legs and flay his forelegs. And, through all of this, Chomper continued to bark. It was the kind of bark that would make a pro wrestler take pause. Chomper's bark made Monique's ribcage vibrate. Eventually, Monique's father asked Mrs. Fletcher and the canine version of a redheaded stepchild to leave. Mrs. Fletcher did so, one hand on the leash, the other over her mouth, saying, "I don't know what's gotten into him." Monique rolled her eyes, along with everyone else in the room.

Soon, the living room cleared out. Mr. Flemming walked Monique and Chase to the door. Mr. Flemming gave Monique a cheek kiss, then addressed Chase. "Take good care of my daughter, Kilbey. Don't make me rough you up like I did with that salesman."

CHAPTER 28

Outside the Flemming house sat an oversized Cadillac. The Hispanic driver held the rear door open for Chase and Monique. The beige vinyl seat was smooth and comfortable. A small TV projected from the middle of the front seat. On the screen were the opening credits for the movie *Bonnie and Clyde*. Chase turned the TV off and said to Monique, "You really do look great tonight."

"And any other time I don't?" Monique smirked.

"You know what I mean."

"I know."

They then exchanged some school gossip. After they exhausted that avenue of conversation, Chase asked Monique why she was a transfer student. She explained that she had to trade in a parochial education for a public one because her mother demanded more alimony. To pay Mrs. Flemming an extra one hundred dollars a month, Monique and her father decided to tighten the budgetary belt and give up Cardinal Dougherty High School, since a catholic education wasn't exactly free.

The topic of Mrs. Flemming's greediness must have made Monique uncomfortable, Chase noted, because she quickly changed the subject.

"Are we picking up any other couples?" Monique asked.

"No," Chase said, "but we're meeting two of my friends there—Nick and Steve. They're going stag. We'll be hanging out with them."

"Oh, okay," Monique said amicably.

Chase glanced out his tinted window. The Caddy climbed up the Cottman Avenue ramp to I-95. Utility poles zipped by as the Caddy accelerated and merged with the stragglers of rush-hour traffic.

"Do you mind if I ask you something?" Monique said.

"Go 'head."

"Do you like animals?"

"Sure, I guess. Never really thought about it. Why do you ask?"

"You seemed kind of tense when Chomper was at my house."

"Chomper? Oh, the German shepherd." Chase cleared his throat. "Well, that's different. I don't like dogs."

"How come?"

Case hesitated. "They scare me."

"I can see why Chomper would, because he's basically a psychopath, but what about cute, cuddly ones like poodles and Chihuahuas?"

"The thing is," Chase began, knuckle rubbing his chin, "when my mom was pregnant with me, about six months into the pregnancy, she was coming back from the corner deli when this 'little pint-sized mutt,' as she calls it, ran across the avenue and began barking at her. She was wearing baggy pants, and the dog chomped on the cuff and wouldn't let go. There were these kids down the block, and they were laughing at her, rolling around in stitches. The dog finally let go of my mom's pant cuff. She doesn't remember why it didn't bite her or anything, but she was pretty shaken up over it."

"And that's why you hate dogs?"

"Sort of. I mean, because of that incident my mom naturally became afraid of dogs, and I think that fear got passed on down to me, you know? I probably should face that f— Hey, look at that!" Chase pointed out Monique's window at the full moon that shined yellow-orange, detailing practically every crook and crevice of the Earth's satellite.

Monique turned back around. "What am I supposed to be looking at, the moon—"

Chase didn't give her a chance to finish. He pecked her on the cheek, then retreated to his side of the seat.

"Sorry," Chase said, beaming, "I couldn't help it. The conversation was getting a little too serious. Besides, you're too beautiful to resist."

He placed his hand over hers. She placed her other hand over his. They grinned at each other.

CHAPTER 29

At the prom, Nick sat at a circular table with Steve, Chase and Monique. The table, situated between a pillar and the kitchen door, had settings for eight, but only the four of them sat here. Occasionally, a classmate would stop by and say hi to Chase, but no one stayed.

At 8 P.M., the servers brought around dinner: filet mignon. Nick's server kept brushing against him and asking if he needed anything else. What was that all about?

Slicing his filet mignon with a dull knife, Nick noticed the DJ had lowered the volume for dinner. Popular instrumentals played, such as "Rockit," "Hooked on Swing," and "Chariots of Fire." It was a vast improvement over the New Wave that had been blaring previously. God, how Nick hated New Wave. It was nothing but a diluted version of punk rock. New Wave extracted the anger and politics of punk so that record companies and radio stations had a *marketable product* they could peddle to suburbia's Polly Whitebreads. And to cause further injury to punk rockers, some genius along the way said, "Hey, let's turn down the guitars and throw in some synthesizers." *Fuck synthesizers*, Nick thought.

Dinner ended a half-hour later. The theme to "Rocky" faded out and the volume rose for Duran Duran's "Is There Something I Should Know?" Nick groaned. The DJ had to have some punk rock in his stacks of tracks. The Circle Jerks' "Jerks on 45" maybe?

The Fixx's "One Thing Leads to Another" was the next New Wave *classic* to blast from the DJ's four-foot-high speakers. Chase led Monique to the dance floor. They flash-danced the night away, while Nick and Steve hovered near the table.

"I don't know how to break this to you," Nick said, "but it looks like we're the only ones here without dates."

Steve frowned.

Noir Reunion

Nick said, "I guess that means you're my bitch tonight."

Steve frowned even more.

"This sucks," Nick said.

"I think I should've stayed home and worked on my computer," Steve said.

"Should've, would've, could've." Nick moved away from the table. "I need to go drain my monstrous snake. Need anything from the bar on my way back?"

Steve shook his head.

Nick strutted across the room, his Converse high-tops giving him an extra bounce.

The bathroom was well lit. It smelled of pine and ammonia, and the floor wasn't sticky like most public bathrooms. Nick stepped up to a urinal and did his business quicker than Speedy Gonzales swiping a piece of cheese. When washing his hands, he looked into the mirror. The bathroom door swung open. In glided his server.

"Hey, how are you?" the server said, moving towards the same urinal Nick had used.

"What's goin' on?" Nick greeted back.

"Nothing much. I'm Jose, by the way."

Nick introduced himself, gazing at Jose. He had broad shoulders and a buzz haircut. He was about eighteen. Nick averted his gaze when Jose zipped up.

"See ya," Nick said, practically running out of the restroom.

"Later."

Nick headed over to the bar and saw that the caterers had dimmed the overhead lights, signifying that the bar was closed.

"What the fuck?" Nick muttered.

"Need help with something?" Jose walked around the bar.

"Yeah," Nick said, "give me a Scotch on the rocks, and go easy on the rocks, if you know what I mean."

Jose smiled, showing a perfect set of pearly whites. "You know I can't serve you."

"That's it! I wanna speak to the manager. Now!" Nick comically banged his fist on the bar.

Jose laughed. "How 'bout some vitamin C-fortified orange juice? Will that hold you over?"

"Make it a double."

Jose made it a single.

Nick stirred the highball glass of OJ with an anorexic straw. Foam clung to the rim of the glass. He finished it in five minutes while talking with Jose about music and movies.

"Want another?" Jose asked.

"Hook me up, barkeep."

When Jose handed off the replenished glass, his thumb touched the web of skin between Nick's thumb and index finger. Nick stared down at Jose's manicured thumb. It felt…nice. Jose withdrew his hand.

"Shouldn't you be getting back to your date?" Jose asked.

"Nah, I came stag," Nick said.

"Why's that?"

Nick shrugged. "There really wasn't anybody I wanted to ask."

Jose nodded. "How's your drink?"

"Good."

Jose scanned under the bar. "Damn, the keg's tapped. Feel like helping me lug one out?"

"Sure," Nick said, although in the back of his mind he wondered why Jose needed a keg. It was a junior prom. Almost everyone here was five years too young to drink legally. Maybe it was a keg of root beer, or maybe Jose wanted to keep the bar stocked for a wedding reception tomorrow.

Nick followed Jose across the floor under the dimmed overhead lights, out of view from the dance floor. The storage closet they aimed for was open. A path of light illuminated the carpet inside the closet.

The closet smelled of mildew and mothballs. Metal shelving lined the walls. Oversized boxes, bottles, cans and jars filled the shelves, except for the one by the door, which was packed with linen. In the center of the room sat a pallet of beer and soda cases. No kegs, though.

Noir Reunion

Nick heard the door click closed. It was now completely dark in here. Nick should've been alarmed, but—surprisingly—he was calmer than Joe Cool skating on thin ice.

"Here," Jose said. He pulled out a penlight and inserted the *eraser* end into a stack of linen. The penlight had enough wattage for Nick to see the outline of Jose's build. "Sorry about not turning on the light," Jose said. "Didn't mean to startle you like that. But I want to talk to you, and if I leave it on, my boss'll come around and see the light's on from underneath the door. Besides, the penlight is bright enough."

"Uh-huh," Nick said.

"Here, sit down."

Nick sat down on a case of Coors Light. He watched Jose unbutton his starchy, white-collar shirt.

"Um…" Nick's voice cracked, his hand tapping his right leg. "What are ya doing?"

"Relax."

Jose stood in front of Nick, blocking the beam from the penlight. Nick noticed Jose's nipples were hard.

"Do anything for you?" Jose asked.

Nick didn't answer. He was so confused. Why was his heart beating quicker than the drum track of an Adolescents song? Any other time he'd pummel a guy for coming on to him. What gives?

"Lean back," Jose whispered in Nick's ear. Nick did as ordered. His butt and back lay on cases of Coors Light, his head and shoulders on a stack of Frank's Orange Soda. The soda cases, an inch higher than the beer cases, acted as a headrest. Nick's neck leaned against a sticky corner of a soda case.

Jose's nose touched Nick's. Nick smelled Polo cologne. Jose kissed Nick's clavicle. Nick closed his eyes for a moment, then opened them. He looked down. Jose kneeled on the Coors Light cases, Nick's hips sandwiched between Jose's legs. Nick closed his eyes again and moaned. Jose's tongue was circling Nick's Adam's apple. Nick started to breathe hard. Jose bit gently into the side of Nick's neck. Involuntarily, Nick brought a hand up. It

99

Johnny Ostentatious

landed on Jose's bicep. Nick caressed the bicep and gasped. Jose's tongue was exploring Nick's ear. Next thing Nick knew, Jose was kissing him. It started as a soft grazing of the lips and soon escalated into a French kiss. Nick clutched Jose's biceps. Jose formed muscles. Nick clutched harder. Jose stopped kissing and said something but Nick didn't hear. Passion drummed inside his head. Nick sat up. Jose rocked on his lap. Nick grabbed Jose by the ears and kissed him hard. Nick felt Jose's nasal breathing bounce off his cheek and towards his shut eyes. Still kissing, Jose removed Nick's tie and cummerbund. When Jose finished unbuttoning Nick's shirt, Nick broke the kiss to catch his breath; his lungs were burning. Nick's hands remained on Jose's ears. He played with Jose's four earrings—two in each ear. Soon, they were both naked. Nick hugged Jose.

Nick panted. "Be gentle."

"Of course," Jose said, entering Nick.

Nick listened to the DJ introduce "Rock 'n' Roll High School" by The Ramones. It played so loud that the shelving to Nick's left rattled. Nick laughed.

Jose growled like a wolf. Nick ran his fingers up and down Jose's back. At Jose's climax, Nick gripped Jose's butt.

Afterwards, Jose lied next to Nick on the beverage cases. Nick wrapped his leg over Jose's waist and rested his hand and head on Jose's sweaty chest. Nick didn't mind Jose's heartbeat thumping in his ear.

Jose pulled out two cigarettes. "Want one?"

"Don't smoke," Nick said.

"You sure?"

"Oh, okay. I guess one won't hurt."

Nick took tiny drags. He didn't cough.

"Whaddya think?" Jose asked.

"It's nice," Nick said. He finished his cigarette and kissed Jose's stubbly cheek. Jose combed Nick's hair with his fingers. Nick purred.

"Ever with a girl?" Jose asked.

"When you say 'with,' do you mean like in the same room?"

"You're so silly. You know what I mean."

"Yeah, I know," Nick said. "I've made out with a few girls. I even had a girlfriend once, but we never had sex. You?"

"Never was with a girl. I like men, not women."

"Have you always known?"

Jose nodded. "Ever since puberty."

Nick sat up and stretched. "Uhhh, I don't think I'll be able to walk for weeks."

"You were great."

"Not bad for a virgin?"

"A born natural," Jose said.

"I feel so groggy. My head hurts. Was there any booze in the OJs you made me?"

"No, but I did slip in some sodium pentothal—it's a truth serum."

"Why'd you do that?"

"Would you've had sex with me if I didn't?"

"Probably not," Nick said.

"There you go." Jose hopped to his feet and began to get dressed. "I need to get back."

"How's this work? Do I see you again or do you only help people come out of the closet?" Nick smirked. "No pun intended."

"I wouldn't mind seeing you again," Jose said.

They exchanged phone numbers, after which Jose kissed Nick on the forehead. With Jose gone, Nick remained on the beer cases, hugging himself. Eventually, he put his tux back on, then limped out the door.

On the dance floor, Nick's classmates boogied to Men At Work's "Down Under."

CHAPTER 30

Chase took Monique's hand. "One more dance?" he asked.
"Oh, all right," she said, mimicking peevishness.
They slow-danced to "Crazy for You" by Madonna. Chase placed his hands on Monique's waist. She rested her wrists on his shoulders. Neither of them led; they moved in tandem. Chase tucked a piece of Monique's hair behind her ear. She smiled up at him.
"Don't know if you're sick of hearing me say this," he whispered in her ear, "but you look out of sight tonight."
Monique grinned. "Keep the compliments coming."
The song faded. Couples returned to their tables. Monique removed her arms from around Chase's neck. He moved his hands from her waist. His right hand slid to her lower back. Bringing her close, his left hand tilted her chin up. He kissed her quickly, yet softly. He sensed her tiptoe, her hands pressed against his chest. He stopped kissing her. He looked down. Her eyes were still closed, lips puckered. He took her hand. She regained composure.
They paraded back their table, staring at each other.

CHAPTER 31

After the prom, Steve, Nick, Chase and Monique drove home in Chase's Camaro. Chase had only had enough money to rent the limo for the ride to the prom. Nick had driven the Camaro to the banquet hall, even though he didn't have a license.

Nick drove now. Steve sat in the passenger seat, while Chase and Monique cuddled in the back. The windows were rolled down, sending in the thickness of the night, a mixture of car exhaust from passing vehicles and springtime humidity.

The Camaro varoomed down Delaware Avenue. Delaware Ave was basically a mile-long industrial park that skirted the Delaware River. Recently, the Philly Mafia started erecting nightclubs on this part of Delaware Ave. Everyone, except the cops, seemed to know the mob owned the nightclubs.

The Camaro stopped at a traffic light. The red light reflected off the windshield, along with the yellow glow of two utility poles.

Steve removed his tux's bow tie. He played with it and glanced up. The traffic light turned green. In the rearview mirror, he saw Chase and Monique holding hands in the backseat. Steve pinched the hook of his bow tie and twirled it around. Fast and hard. Hard and fast.

She belongs with me, Steve thought. *I'm the one who loves her, not Chase.*

For the past month, Steve had scolded himself for procrastinating over asking Monique to the prom, but the right moment had never presented itself. Either Monique was gallivanting the school halls with a group of girls, or if she was alone, he didn't feel like approaching her. Now he was paying the price for his procrastination. Chase had taken advantage of Steve's habitual hesitation and had gotten to Monique first. It wasn't fair! Chase never had problems with girls. He seemed to have a special sense of knowing whether they were attracted to him or not. *Stupid jerk.*

Steve's wrist was beginning to hurt. He stopped swinging his bow tie. His thumb and index finger were purple from pinching the hook. A tiny drop of blood dripped from his finger. The blood crossed the valleys of his fingerprints and crept under his fingernail.

"You okay?" Nick asked.

Steve nodded.

"You seem a little sullen tonight," Nick said. "More than usual."

"I'm fine."

"Want me to put on some punk rock?"

"No," Steve said emphatically.

"You sure? Drexel University has got this kick-ass show on Saturday nights. It's called Uniquely Untalented. It's hosted by this student there who calls himself Mike the Kike."

"I don't want to listen to any of that…stuff." Steve almost said shit, but caught himself. He took pride in the fact that he was one of the few teenagers who didn't curse.

"You sure?" Nick said, smirking. "I don't mind putting it on. It's no trouble. Hey, maybe they'll play some Descendents. They're pretty cool. You'll like 'em. They play punk with a huge dose of pop. A lot of their songs are about girl trouble. You know, being dumped or not being able to get a date."

Steve nodded, wondering why Nick reeked of Polo cologne. Nick hated cologne, always claiming it was superficial and a sign of vanity. Also, why was Nick glowing like a freaking firefly? He wasn't like that before the prom.

Steve stopped speculating about Nick. He froze. Slurping emanated from the backseat. Chase and Monique were kissing. Eventually they stopped and started whispering. Monique muffled a titter, burrowing her face into Chase's chest. Steve formed a fist. *I hate them, I hate them, I hate them, I hate them.*

Nick coughed into his shoulder. "That prom was pretty beat, huh?"

"Yes," Steve said.

"I still can't believe they played The Ramones. That's pretty fucking wild."

Steve shrugged and glanced at the backseat. Monique's dress was pulled up to her knees. Chase caressed Monique's shin while talking to her.

Just you wait, Steve thought. *You'll be sorry. One day, I'll make you all sorry.*

CHAPTER 32

"What the hell?" Nick said.

Delaware Ave was blocked off. Police barricades prohibited traffic in both directions from continuing onward. Cars were turning down side streets.

Nick didn't turn at first. He was too busy scoping out the crime scene. Looked like a brawl had broken out in front of the Stardust nightclub. One erstwhile club-goer lied facedown in the middle of the avenue on the double-yellow lane divider. Several feet away sat a half-dozen meatheads. The cops had broken them up into couples. Two meatheads each were handcuffed together, back to back. Girls stood on the sidewalk, held back by flatfoots. The meatheads were obviously their beaus. The girls called the cops cock-suckers. Each girl wore a tight, low-cut dress, showcasing breast implants.

Nick quit observing the scene. He steered the Camaro to follow a procession of cars down a side street. Most of the cars turned at the first intersection, but Nick didn't. He kept driving. He was pretty sure he knew a shortcut somewhere around here. He'd remember it if he drove around a little bit.

Five minutes later, they were lost.

Chase popped his head between the front seats. "Where are we?"

"Damned if I know," Nick said.

They seemed to be in an industrial park. On both sides were factories: a six-story one on the right, and a ten-story one on the left. The six-story factory had a barbed wire fence. The ten-story factory had a dock the size of the Titanic; parked there were several eighteen-wheelers. Both factories appeared inactive—no night shift.

Chase returned to the backseat. Nick lightheartedly asked Steve, "How the hell did we drive into an industrial park?"

Steve shrugged.

"Yo," Nick said, continuing to coast the Camaro down the curvy road, "you sure I didn't miss anything? Did we go through a gate or pass a security guard, or something?"

Steve shook his head.

Chase said, "I've never even been down here before. I bet my dad would know where we are."

"Well," Nick joked, "that's all well and good, but he ain't here, is he? He's probably passed out somewhere in some brothel."

"Screw you, dude," Chase said amiably. "You know my dad would never cheat on my mom."

"We'll let the divorce court decide that, you—you naïve young pup."

Monique giggled.

"What?" Chase said.

"You two are something else."

Nick glanced back. "So what are you trying to say, we're retarded?"

"Nick!" Steve said.

Nick turned around to see a dead end quickly approaching; it consisted of a brick wall with a guardrail jutting out. Nick hit the brakes. The Camaro came within a half-inch of the guardrail's red reflectors.

"Oh my God!" Monique said.

"That's it," Chase said, "pull over at the next payphone. I'm calling the DMV and telling them never to give you a license."

"Yeah, yeah, yeah," Nick said. "You're killing me, Bob Hope To Die."

"Seriously, dude," Chase said, "let me drive."

"Nah, sit back there and keep swapping smooches with your honey. But do me a favor, though, try and keep the slurping sounds down to a minimum."

Chase laughed.

Nick made a U-turn and drove towards the ten-story factory.

"What are you doing?" Chase asked.

"Wanna check something out." Nick parked next to a white

van that looked as if it hadn't been washed since Ira Einhorn fled Philadelphia for France. Nick cut the engine, hopped out (surprisingly, he didn't ache too much from the lovemaking session with Jose) and strutted over to the dock. He bent down to pick up what had caught his eye, and brought it back to the Camaro.

"What is it?" Chase asked.

"Cable," Nick answered, holding it up. It was a foot long, two inches thick and weighed about five pounds. At the two ends you could see the one hundred copper coils that made up the cable. The coils stayed in place thanks to grey rubber insulation.

"What do you need that for?" Monique asked.

"Weapon."

"I don't think I like you having that in my car," Chase said.

Monique asked, "Don't the police consider that a lethal weapon?"

"We won't get pulled over," Nick said. "I'll be extra careful."

Suddenly, headlights pierced the darkness inside the Camaro. Nick tucked the cable under his seat.

CHAPTER 33

Chase leaned forward. "What is it?"

"I don't know," Nick said, "but I doubt it's good."

The headlights no longer shined inside the Camaro, and Chase couldn't see the car that the headlights belonged to. The white van the Camaro was parked next to blocked Chase's view.

"See anything?" Chase asked Nick.

"No, that van's in my way. C'mon." Nick opened the door. The interior light clicked on.

"What?" Chase asked.

"We're going to check it out," Nick said.

Chase noticed Nick held the cable close to his chest, as if a soldier hugging a rifle.

"Okay," Chase said. He turned to Monique. "We'll be right back."

Monique nodded. She didn't seem scared at all. Chase liked that.

Nick held the door open for Chase. Since Chase was sitting on the driver side of the back seat, he didn't have to climb over Monique. Before hopping out, Chase patted Steve on the shoulder.

Chase and Nick stood at the Camaro's front bumper. The van sat in front of them. (Nick had parked the Camaro perpendicular to the van.)

Nick took off his tuxedo jacket. Chase asked what he was doing. Nick explained that he didn't want to be seen. That's why he was putting his black tux jacket on backwards, so the lapels and buttons were on his back. Wearing the jacket this way covered his bright-white shirt. Chase put his jacket on backwards, too.

Chase followed Nick. They tiptoed towards the front of the van. The van was at an angle that let them peer through the rolled-down windows and see what was happening on the industrial park street. Chase was glad the windows were rolled down. They were probably filthy like the windshield. Cigarette smoke had given the windshield a brownish tint. The middle of it sported a BB hole. Somebody had placed a wad of pink chewing gum in the hole. The May heat had liquefied the gum. The gum dangled by a thread, the bulk of the gum hovering an inch above the dashboard littered with styrofoam cups, empty cigarette packs and Joe Bazooka bubble gum wrappers.

Chase quit taking in the details of the van. He focused on the scene ahead.

In the middle of the street, two idling cars faced each other. They were ten feet apart. Both cars' headlights were on. Chase assumed the car closest to him, a Lexus, was the one whose headlights had shined in his Camaro. It must have had been making a U-turn or something.

The other car was a Mercedes. Its high beams were on. This prevented Chase from making out any of the figures that stood to the side of both cars.

Somebody stood in front of the Mercedes, blocking the passenger-side headlight. Hands on hips, he yelled to the back of the Mercedes.

From the rear of the Mercedes waddled a miniature man. Miniature couldn't have been any more than four feet. He carried a wooden table that was almost as tall as himself. He set the table up between the two cars, then scuttled away as if a rodent released from captivity.

Two men, one from each car, approached the table. Chase couldn't make out either of them. Thanks to the glaring headlights, they were nothing but silhouettes.

The two men each placed a suitcase on the table.

"Drug deal," Nick whispered to Chase.

Chase saw that each man had placed his suitcase on the table with the handle facing away from him, so the other man could open it. The suitcases were so large, they both hung a couple inches over the side of the table. Each man tried subtly to maneuver his suitcase to make up for the two-inch overhang. That went on for about a minute. It finally ended when two people coughed, one from each entourage.

"This is some fucked-up shit," Nick whispered.

Chase nodded.

Simultaneously, each man opened his suitcase. Chase saw one of the suitcases contained enough cocaine to satiate Martin Scorsese for several years. Chase couldn't see inside the other suitcase.

"What do you want to do?" Chase asked Nick.

"Wait till they finish up and split, then we'll skedaddle."

CHAPTER 34

Monique played with her choker necklace. Chase and Nick had been gone for ten minutes, and in that time, Steve hadn't uttered one word. He hadn't even turned around. He just stared at his lap, the back of his hairy, pimply neck facing her.

Steve's behavior puzzled Monique. She was used to boys hitting on her. She couldn't remember the last time a boy ignored her.

Monique was especially perplexed by Steve's behavior because she knew he liked her. He spent more time in biology class staring at her than the blackboard. Why was he ignoring her now? *He's probably shy. Or maybe he's intimidated by girls.*

"Steve?"

"Yes?" he said without turning around.

"Are you okay?"

"Mm-hmm." Pregnant pause. "Why do you ask?" His voice cracked on the word you.

"You're very quiet," Monique said.

Steve turned around, not fully, but enough so Monique could see his face. He didn't make eye contact.

"Did you have a good time tonight?" Monique asked.

Shrug.

"I had a great time," Monique said, feeling as if she were talking to herself. "It was a lot better than my soph hop. That was a nightmare. Not one thing went right. The boy I went with was getting over the flu, and halfway through the night, somebody pulled the fire alarm, so we all had to leave the hall for a half-hour. Then it started raining…"

"Uh-huh," Steve said.

Monique didn't say anything else for a couple minutes. She listened to the engines of the two cars that Chase and Nick were checking out. Exhaust from one of the cars crept through the crack in Monique's window. That smell was occasionally overpowered by the stench of a nearby Dumpster.

Monique removed her shoes. Even though the heels weren't that high, they were killing her. It was a shame. She liked them. Bought them at Thom McAn while out shopping on one Saturday afternoon with her dad.

"So, Steve, was your girlfriend at the prom tonight?" Monique winced as soon as the question left her lips. What a lame attempt at small talk.

"I don't date," Steve said. He made eye contact.

Monique froze. Steve's eyes were the saddest she had ever seen; they hinted of a scarred childhood. Monique knew that no matter what Steve did, he would never fit in. For the rest of his life, he would be a social misfit. Throughout adulthood, the schoolyard bullies would continue to push him around. And the girls at school dances would grow up into women who would still shun him. Steve was that rare breed of male who was both ugly and boring. Monique hated to admit it, even to herself, but it was true. Usually, when a person is unattractive, they have a great personality, or if they're boring, the gene game compensates by granting them with the beauty of a Greek god or Roman goddess. But the tides of fate had cursed Steve in both respects. Monique felt a huge amount of pity for him. She felt so bad that if he had asked her to the prom before Chase, she might have gone with him, just to boost his self-esteem. She might have even initiated a one-night stand. No, bad idea. That would've only resulted in him following her around like an attention-starved puppy.

Steve shifted in his seat, his cheeks coloring ruby red. Monique realized that pity was the reason Chase palled around with Steve. She thought it was a charitable gesture on Chase's part. It made her like him more.

Monique crossed her arms. "Why don't you date?"

"I don't know, I just don't." Steve shrugged, as if for emphasis.

"Well, was there anybody you wanted to ask to the prom?"

Nod.

"Who?" Monique uncrossed her arms.

Steve didn't say anything for a few moments. He stared at his lap. The blushing of his cheeks inched towards his temples. A trickle of sweat ran down his forehead, absorbed by his left eyebrow. Finally, he grunted a word: a syllable. It was so guttural, Monique couldn't make it out.

"What's that?" she asked.

"You," Steve said. "You. I wanted to ask you out." He was shaking.

I knew it, Monique thought. "Why didn't you?"

Shrug. "You went with Chase."

"But you never asked."

"How could I!" Steve said. "Every time I wanted to, you were standing around, giggling with your stupid friends!"

Monique shrank back into her seat, hugging herself. Steve's tone brimmed with the anger of a wife-beater.

Steve turned back around to face the windshield. Monique looked out the window, wishing Chase would return soon.

CHAPTER 35

Nick froze. A member from one of the entourages had spotted the Camaro. The entourage member marched towards it.

"Shit," Nick said, gripping the cable.

"What are we going to do?" Chase asked.

"Get down."

They ducked under the van's driver-side window. Nick took off his tux jacket. Chase did the same. They sat on their butts and feet, chins resting on their knees.

Nick dropped to the ground. Lying prone, he watched the entourage member stride towards the van. The entourage member wore alligator-skin shoes and black pants with sharp pleats.

Nick sensed his back muscles twitch. He shifted slightly and inadvertently let go of his weapon, the cable.

He gasped.

The cable rolled under the van faster than the rolling boulder in the beginning of *Raiders of the Lost Ark*. One end of the cable tapped the rear passenger-side tire. That didn't slow it down. The cable kept on trucking until it reached the entourage member's foot. The entourage member raised his foot and stopped the cable by treading on it. Nick heard the entourage member cock an automatic weapon, its sound echoing. Nick sprang off his hands and knees, returning to his former position: sitting on his butt and feet.

"Let's get out of here," Chase said.

"How?" Nick said.

"We'll drive through."

Nick didn't reply. He realized he was practically hyperventilating. He tried to control his breathing. When it was finally under control, he saw the entourage member's automatic rifle peeking around the back of the van. Then, the entourage member's hand came into view. His finger touched the trigger, ready to fire at the smallest provocation. Suddenly, he stopped.

Johnny Ostentatious

Somebody near the table yelled, "Yo, what's he doing?"

The entourage member near Nick said in Spanish, "Checking something out."

From the table, somebody shouted in English, "It's a trick!"

"Run!" somebody else said.

Nick watched the men at the table grab their suitcases and dash back to their cars. In unison, they barked the same order (one in English, one in Spanish): "Shoot 'em!"

Gunfire broke out, lighting up the sky.

The entourage member near Nick and Chase peeped his head around the van. Nick saw he had a Barry Manilow nose and skin the color of an Aztec. Nick also saw Aztec's automatic rifle was an Uzi.

Seeing that Nick and Chase were unarmed, Aztec paraded around the back of the van with the cockiness of a state trooper. He motioned the Uzi at them.

"Get up," he said in Spanish.

Nick stood up. Chase didn't know Spanish, so Nick translated with a head movement.

Aztec scratched the side of his head with the front sight of the Uzi. His coal-colored hair, pulled back into a ponytail, was greasier than McDonald's French fries. On his fingers were gold, onyx and silver rings—at least two rings on each finger.

Nick couldn't believe a real drug dealer swaggered in front of him. Aztec looked like a stereotypical character from *Miami Vice*. Maybe there was truth in some stereotypes.

Aztec finished scratching his head with the Uzi. Nick was amazed the shootout on the other side of the van didn't faze Aztec because Nick could barely hear himself breathe.

"Who else is with you?" Aztec said in English, in a clipped Midwestern accent.

"No one," Nick said. "Just us."

Chase glanced at the Camaro. *Fuck,* Nick thought, *did Aztec catch that?*

"You know what?" Aztec flashed white teeth, a gap between his upper-right cuspid and premolar. "Know what I think? I think you're all lying. I think your two girlfriends are in there. Eh, prom boys?"

Aztec said something else, but Nick couldn't make it out. The gunfire seemed to increase in decibels by the minute. Nick's ribcage was vibrating as if at a heavy metal concert.

"There's no one in there," Chase said, shouting over the gunfire. "Only us."

"Let's go." Aztec licked his lips. "Move."

Nick and Chase turned around to face the Camaro. Nick relaxed slightly. Monique and Steve weren't visible. Good, maybe they had ducked out of the Camaro and were now hiding in the factory. Nick hoped so. Who knew what Aztec would do if he saw Monique.

Nick and Chase stepped towards the passenger side of the Camaro.

"Stop!" Aztec said. "You, come here."

Nick approached Aztec, his gaze never leaving the drug dealer's. Nick stopped three feet from Aztec.

"Closer," Aztec said.

Nick moved one foot closer. Aztec, Uzi pointing at Nick's chest, used his free hand to grab the punk rocker's neck. Nick tried to remain calm, but he jumped at the initial contact. How could he not? Aztec's fingers were colder than a vampire's heart.

Nick withdrew his attention from Aztec for a moment. The gunfight between the two entourages was quieting down.

Nick shivered. A hangnail from Aztec's thumb grazed Nick's earlobe.

"So you're the tough one, eh?" Aztec said.

"If you say so."

"That's right. I do say so. I'm in charge. How's that feel, punk?"

"Like I'm hangin' out at Xanadu."

Aztec sneered. "You think you're funny? How's this?"

He jabbed the Uzi into Nick's sternum. Nick did his best not to wince.

"How's that, Robin Williams? Let's see you smirk now."

Johnny Ostentatious

Nick played stoic. Aztec pulled the Uzi back.

"Stupid fucking white kids," Aztec said. "You all make me sick. Walking around in your fancy houses and nice cars. It's because of you and your racist parents that I'm the way I am. You probably think I been a felon most of my life, right? Well, listen to this. I was a straight-A student all through grade school and high school. I wanted to go to college in the worst way, but you know what, no *institution of higher learning* would take me. One school even said I'd be 'best served with taking the civil-service test.'" Aztec snickered. "So now I make my living selling drugs to spoiled little white kids like yourself. I figure it's not such a bad *career path*. After all, every time one of you OD's or comes around begging for some free blow, I know I'm the one in control. Plus, I make more money in one year than all of you will make in a lifetime. And you know what else?"

Aztec's knee shot for Nick's groin. Nick fell on his back, curled into a ball and closed his eyes. The pain emanating from his family jewels reverbed throughout his entire body. To make matters worse, Aztec tried kicking Nick in the stomach, though the punk rocker's hands deflected most of those kicks. Then, abruptly, the kicking stopped.

"Hold it, hero," Nick heard Aztec say to Chase. Nick opened his teary eyes to see the blurry image of his best friend. Chase had leapt onto the Camaro's engine hood. Aztec pointed the Uzi at Chase's chest. Chase slid off the hood and returned to his position on the passenger side of the Camaro.

"Get up," Aztec said to Nick. Nick did so, but with great effort. Eyes squeezed shut, he tried using the driver-side mirror to help pull himself up. The pain in his groin was so incredibly excruciating that it was taking him forever to stand.

"Hurry up!" Aztec said in Spanish. He poked Nick in the side with the Uzi. Nick opened his eyes. He stood, clutching the Camaro's antenna. *Thank God.* The groin pain was abating.

"Open the door," Aztec said. "Slowly."

Nick pulled the driver-side door handle. The door was sticking. He pulled a litter harder. The tightening of stomach muscles brought a resurgence of the groin pain, but only for a second.

Nick opened the car door. Steve sat on the floor, crouched under the glovebox. His eyes bulged like a panicky rabbit.

"Come on," Nick said kindly.

Steve, sobbing, slid out, climbing clumsily over the gearshift and driver seat. Aztec forced Steve to lay facedown on the ground next to the front, driver-side tire.

Nick cocked his head. Was the gunfight over? He hadn't heard anything for awhile.

"Looks like we got ourselves a little baby here," Aztec said, referring to Steve. "Are you a pussy, my man? A little girly-man?"

Steve continued to sob.

"Get on your hands and knees," Aztec said.

Sluggishly, Steve did so.

"Since you're a little crybaby, you must be a little bitch, eh? You probably take it in the ass, eh, little girly-man?"

Aztec inserted the Uzi between Steve's butt cheeks. Still clothed, Steve shook as if naked during a snowstorm. He looked up at Nick. The tears streaming down Steve's cheeks made the punk rocker look away.

Aztec pushed the Uzi, as if he hoped to burst through the seam of Steve's pants. "How'd you like a round up your colon, girly-man?"

A ripping sound filled the air. Aztec stepped back. Nick smirked. Steve's bowels and bladder emptied out. The stench of urine and feces was overwhelming.

"Get up," Aztec said.

Steve did as ordered. Fecal matter oozed down his leg, onto one of his shoes. Urine soaked the front of his pants.

Aztec glared at Steve and walked around to the passenger side of the Camaro. "You," he said to Chase, "pull down the seat."

Chase opened the passenger door. Nick, still standing on the driver side, held his breath. He saw where this was going.

Chase pulled the front seat forward. To Nick, it sounded like a roller coaster clacking up an incline.

"Very nice," Aztec said.

Nick, unable to see inside the Camaro, assumed Monique was lying on the backseat floor.

"Out," Aztec said.

Chase helped Monique out of the Camaro. Her face was whiter than pure heroin.

"Let go of him," Aztec told Monique.

Both of her hands were wrapped around Chase's left hand. She slowly let go.

"Good," Aztec said. "Turn around."

Monique twirled with the trepidation of a scared schoolgirl. Nick wondered if that was how an aspiring girl singer moved when in the bedroom of a record company executive.

"You're a hot little one," Aztec said. "Anyone ever tell you that?"

Monique nodded imperceptibly.

"Get on the trunk." Aztec unbuttoned his shirt. A gold crucifix hung between his nipples.

Monique didn't move. She looked to Chase, then to Nick.

"On the trunk!" Aztec pointed the Uzi at Nick and Chase. "Which one's your date? This one?" Chase. "This one?" Nick.

Monique shook her head.

"Which one, bitch!"

Monique hesitated, then pointed at Chase.

"Tell her," Aztec said to Chase. "Tell her to get on top of the trunk."

But Chase didn't need to. Monique moved for the trunk, the gravel stones audible under her bare feet.

"I don't believe this," Chase said, looking away.

"Be cool, my man," Aztec said in Spanish.

Chase started pacing.

"I said, be cool," Aztec said in English.

Chase stopped pacing.

Nick couldn't bear to look at Monique being violated. Arms crossed, he turned around to see the result of the gunfight.

Members from both entourages lay on the ground, bleeding on the asphalt. It seemed everyone was dead. Wait, one was getting up. He didn't appear harmed. Nick watched him approach. His gait was determined, yet unhurried.

Nick whirled around. Aztec hadn't attacked Monique yet. He was still drooling over the sight of her in the prom dress. She lay on the trunk, back against the rear window.

"Chico!" said the approaching man.

Nick's heart cut off in mid-beat. He knew that voice.

CHAPTER 36

Chase saw a Hispanic man approach. He sported four earrings, two in each ear, and wore black pants and a white shirt, both speckled with blood. He held two guns. One looked to be a Glock 9mm, the other a Smith & Wesson 38.

"Jose?" Nick said.

"Hello, Nick," Jose said nonchalantly, as if running into an old friend at a cocktail party. "What are you doing here? Shouldn't you be enjoying your night of passage, getting laid somewhere?" He winked.

Chico (Aztec) unbuttoned his pants. "Get the fuck out of here. I got some business to finish up."

Jose's cordial manner vanished. "What the hell do you think you're doing? 'Cause of you, everybody's dead."

"Hey, I ain't the one that panicked."

"Maybe, but while you're over here harassing these kids, we were fighting for our lives."

"Fuck off," Chico said.

"Okay. You had your fun terrorizing these poor little white kids. Let's go."

"I ain't finished."

"Yes, you are," Jose said.

Chico stepped away from Monique. He buckled his pants with one hand, waving his Uzi around with the other. "Always giving orders. Always correcting my manners. Always telling us what to do. I'm sick of it! You hear me? It's time for some new blood."

Jose strode up to Chico's face, the tips of their shoes touching. "You think you can do better?" Jose said. "I got news for you, *homey*, you wouldn't last a week in my position. You know why? 'Cause you have no respect for our traditions."

"I don't care! It's time for a change."

"Okay. What should we change?"

"First," Chico said, "I'd give myself a bigger cut."

"What?" Jose stepped back.

"Yeah. More cash..." Chico pointed his Barry Manilow nose at Monique. "...more fringe benefits."

"White women? Why in the world would you want that? You have enough trouble satisfying Latino women."

"Fuck you, faggot."

Jose smiled. "Was that supposed to hurt my feelings?"

"No, this is."

Chico fired his Uzi. Chase, Nick, Steve and Monique ducked. Bullets from Chico's Uzi sprayed in an arc. Jose rose his guns a second too late. Bullets from the Uzi pierced Jose's chest and stomach. Jose stumbled back, pulling the triggers of his guns. Two bullets shot Chico, one in each eye. Jose and Chico fell to the ground in unison. Chico, on his back, didn't move. Jose tried sitting up. Nick ran over to him.

Chase helped Monique off the trunk. He hugged her. She hugged him back.

Steve still stood next to the driver-side door. He quivered.

Chase and Monique broke their hug. Chase asked Steve, "You okay?"

Steve didn't respond.

Chase felt Monique grasp his hand. He wrapped his free arm around her and watched Nick hold Jose in his arms. Jose whispered into Nick's ear, then died.

CHAPTER 37

Nibbling on his nails, Steve trembled. He stared down at Chico. The drug dealer's eyes no longer existed. Blood gushed from the sockets, despite the body lying supinely. Steve looked away. The gravity-defying blood didn't bother him. What did was the left eyelid dangling by a thread from the outer corner of the eye. The lid's underside faced Steve. The corner of the lid that had neighbored with the nose now made friendly with a mole on Chico's temple. Blood darkened the eyelashes so much that it looked like clumpy mascara.

Rage consumed Steve. Rage for being unpopular at school. Rage for going to the prom stag. Rage for missing his opportunity to date Monique. And rage for being humiliated by Chico.

The rage made Steve's throat hurt. He attempted to swallow, but it came back up as a scream.

Steve kicked Chico in the side three times with his right foot. He stopped and switched to his left foot. That was when Chase grabbed him from behind, putting him in a full nelson, pulling him away from the corpse.

"Easy," Chase said. "Easy, easy."

Steve, going slack in Chase's hold, breathed heavily through his nose. He smelled Monique's perfume on Chase.

"Let me go!" Steve said.

"Not until you calm down. Okay?"

"Okay."

"Okay," Chase said.

Steve didn't feel Chase release him. He was too busy gaping at Nick.

Nick kissed Jose lightly on his blood-red lips.

CHAPTER 38

In the Camaro, Nick and Steve sat in the backseat, while Monique was in the front with Chase. Monique looked at everyone. Their tired faces reminded her of a picture her father kept on his nightstand. It featured his platoon after they'd emerged victorious from a Vietcong ambush outside of 1967 Da Nang. None of her father's fellow soldiers had died during the battle, but all thirteen had the look of men who'd taken a ten-hour tour of duty through Hell and were mentally scarred by the madness of Lucifer's subterranean world.

Monique took stock of herself. She didn't look that bad, considering she was almost raped. Nonetheless, her hands, resting on her lap, wouldn't stop shaking.

Chase started the Camaro. He coasted around Jose and Chico's bodies. Next up were the idling Mercedes and Lexus.

"Stop," Nick said.

"What?" Chase said, hitting the brakes. The force of the stop made Monique slide forward.

"Let me out," Nick said.

Monique got out and pulled the seat up. Nick hopped out. He stepped over a couple dead bodies and stopped when he reached the miniature man. Miniature was dead like the others, except he clutched a suitcase. Nick yanked the suitcase from Miniature's rigor mortis grip, then returned to the Camaro backseat.

"What is it?" Chase asked.

"The money," Nick said. "Jose told me to take it."

Chase nodded and took his foot off the brake. The Camaro left the crime scene.

CHAPTER 39

Homicide detective Bruno Savage was driving his 1974 Plymouth Scamp through Port Richmond (a working-class borough of Philadelphia) when he saw someone familiar at the intersection of Allegheny Avenue and Richmond Street. Savage pulled over—disregarding traffic patterns—and parallel-parked his Plymouth between a truck cab and a Thunderbird on blocks.

"Traci!" Savage yelled out his window.

A fourteen-year-old girl in a McDonald's uniform froze. Savage strutted across the street, trench coat flapping. He grabbed Traci by the arm and pulled her into an alley between two stores that were closed. It was well past midnight.

Traci Miller was five feet tall, had a dozen pimples on her chin and forehead, and was more endowed than most girls her age.

Savage slammed Traci against a brick wall. Red brick dust floated up his nose. He snorted and spit out the dust.

"What the fuck do you think you're doing?" Savage asked.

"Going home," Traci said, eyes down.

"Going home? Going home! The night's young. If anything, you should be going out."

"I been meaning to talk to you about that, Bruno," Traci said. "I don't wanna do it no more. I wanna go straight."

Savage let go of Traci's arm and chuckled. "You want to go straight, huh? Well, it's a little late for that, ain't it?"

"Bruno, please." Traci laid a hand on Savage's South of the Border T-shirt.

Savage formed a fist and with the speed of Cassius Clay clocked Traci on the side of the head. She dropped to the ground, onto a trash bag. Blood dripped out of her ear and onto one of her hoop earrings.

"You wanna go straight?" Savage shouted. "How's this for an answer? No!"

"Bruno, please." Traci was kneeling, reaching for his leg.

"Get up, you fuckin' cunt."

Traci hugged Savage's leg. "Bruno, please. I don't wanna turn tricks no more."

"I said get up, you fuckin' cunt-swab."

Savage pulled Traci up, clasped his hand around her throat and pushed her against the wall. Tears ran down her cheeks. She reeked of fat-fryer grease.

"You listen to me, you little fuckin' whore." Savage's free hand pointed an index finger at Traci. "You *are* going to quit that job at Mc-key-dees and hike that little drop-out ass of yours down to Frankford Ave and start earning again. You hear me? Or I'll make an anonymous call, and that little toddler of yours will go into a foster home. Understand?"

Savage let go of Traci. She hunched over, hands covering her face. He turned his back to her and stared at the alley's dead-end.

"I'll go to the cops," Traci muttered.

Savage whipped around. "What did you say?"

Traci shook her head forcefully. "I didn't say nothing. I'm sorry. I wasn't thinking."

"Let's get something straight," Savage said, hands on hips, trench coat open, big belly exposed. "You were the one who murdered the father of your child."

"It was suicide!"

"Traci, Traci, Traci. No court is going to believe that. Now, he may have been alone when he hanged himself, but let's face it, you might as well have been in that room, tying that noose."

"No, no. I was at my mother's."

"Don't matter," Savage said, snorting.

A year ago, Traci decided that what she wanted more than anything was to have a baby. To make this dream a reality, she seduced an insecure loner at school. After the night of lovemaking, he told her he wanted to be her boyfriend. She blew him off, but he was persistent. So, pregnant with child, Traci began sleeping around. The loner got the message. Coincidentally, he committed suicide the minute the baby was born.

"I'm so sorry," Traci said, eyes glassy.

"Whatever," Savage said.

"Please."

"You have a choice," Savage said. "Either get out there and hustle, or go to jail and possibly get the death penalty."

"Can't I keep my job at McDonald's?"

"What good is that going to do? The money you owe me each month would take you close to a year to make at that fuckin' grease trap. Now get out of my sight."

Traci sprinted out of the alley.

CHAPTER 40

"Look out!" Monique said.

Chase already saw the teenager in the McDonald's uniform running across the atypically quiet Allegheny Avenue. Chase slammed the brakes. The Camaro screeched, rear pulling to the left. Smelling burning rubber, Chase held on tight to the steering wheel, careful not to bang against any parked cars.

The Camaro stopped within six inches of the girl. She didn't even pause. Just kept on running.

"Holy shit," Nick said from the backseat, "what the fuck just happened?"

"A girl ran out in the middle of the street," Monique said. It was the first time Chase heard fear in Monique's voice.

"Where'd she come from?" Nick asked.

"I don't know," Chase said. "That alley, I think."

Chase pointed and saw a man exit the alley in question. The man was about six feet tall, wore a trench coat, and had a bushy moustache, as well as wiry facial stubble. He slammed his hands on Chase's rolled-down window. Chase noticed the undersides of the man's fingernails were filled with black grime.

"Going kind of fast, weren't you, pretty boy?" the man said.

Chase glanced at his foot on the brake. The gas pedal was so close. All he had to do was move his foot a couple inches to the right.

"Don't even think about it," the man said, reaching into his pocket. "Bruno Savage. Philadelphia Police." He flashed his badge. "Mind telling me why you were speeding?"

"I wasn't," Chase said, unsure if he was telling the truth. "That girl came out of nowhere."

Savage pulled out a flashlight. He shined it on Steve and Nick in the backseat. Chase prayed Nick didn't have the suitcase on his lap. Hopefully, he had put it on the floor when they left the industrial park.

Savage shined the flashlight on Steve. "What is *that* stench?" Savage asked.

Chase exaggeratedly sniffed the air. "We're pretty close to the slaughterhouse. Maybe that's what you smell."

Savage grunted. "Maybe."

Chase relaxed, grateful his acting—no, his lying—had fooled the cop. The last thing the four of them needed was to explain why Steve had urinated and defecated on himself, and why they had a suitcase full of money in the backseat.

Savage's flashlight beam fell on Monique. "Prom night?" he asked.

"Yes," Chase said.

Savage pulled out a handheld notepad. "License and registration."

Chase tried to remain calm. He dug around in the glovebox and without too much trouble found his license and registration. He handed them over. Savage jotted down some information; Chase couldn't see what. Savage handed back the two cards. Chase didn't put them back in the glovebox. His thumb played with a folded-up corner of the registration.

"All of youse," Savage said, "out of the car."

Nick groaned. Chase dropped his registration.

"Problem?" Savage asked.

Monique leaned over, hand resting on Chase's thigh. "It's just that it's been a long night, sir," she said. "We're really very tired and would like to go home and get some sleep."

Savage ran one of his large hands over his nose and mouth. "Okay. I'll let youse go this time, but if I ever see any of you again, I won't be so nice. Capeesh?"

"Capeesh," Chase and his friends chorused.

CHAPTER 41

Savage watched the Camaro pull away, then hopped into his Plymouth. It took five tries before his car finally turned over. He pulled out of the parking spot, thinking of the money that Traci was earning for him. Soon he would be able to afford a new car and get rid of this piece of shit.

Sitting at a stoplight, Savage turned on his police radio. A crime scene was close by, at an industrial park. Savage arrived ten minutes later. He would have arrived sooner, but his Plymouth stalled at every red light.

Savage parked his Plymouth next to Tim Burns. Burns was head of the forensic unit. Ever since they'd met on the job in 1979, they'd disliked each other more than political rivals in a primary race. Savage thought Burns was a pencil-neck geek who worshipped rules and regulations, while Burns thought Savage ranked lower than flesh-eating bacteria.

"What's up?" Savage said.

"Trying to figure out what happened here." Burns motioned at the carnage on the ground.

"All dead?"

"Apparently."

"How many?"

"Thirteen at last count."

"Drugs?"

Burns nodded. Savage sighed nasally.

"That's real attractive," Burns said.

"What?"

"You now have a booger dangling from that scruff you call a moustache."

Savage ran a hand down his face. The snot was yellow-green and clung to the wart on his ring finger. Savage wiped it on his Plymouth and wondered if the snot was visible when he was harassing those kids in the Camaro.

Johnny Ostentatious

Burns shook his head. Savage pretended not to notice and lit up a cigar.

One of the rookies approached. Richard Avila was about twenty and looked, at least to Savage, like he belonged on a Spanish soap opera. (A suitable analogy beings Avila was quite the Casanova, if you believed precinct gossip.)

"Well, well, well," Avila said, carrying a clipboard. "Look who it is. The one voted most likely to be diseased."

"What's up, Ponch."

"Ponch?"

"Yeah," Savage blew cigar smoke out of the corner of his mouth. "You know, Ponch. CHiPs. Mr. California Highway Patrol. That's who you are. Ponch. Riding around on a motorcycle 'cause you like to have something vibrating between your legs."

"Whatever," Avila said, face blushing slightly beneath his copper skin.

"At least that's what your mom told me last night while I was fucking her up the ass with your dead dad's dick."

Avila threw down the clipboard with the theatrics of a melodramatic Shakespearean actor. Savage didn't flinch as Avila pressed his firm, rookie stomach against Savage's veteran, big belly.

"What chu say about my mom?"

"Nothing, except when she came, she said I fucked her better and harder than you ever did."

"You fucking—"

Burns slid an arm between Savage and Avila. "Break it up, break it up!"

"You are so dead!" Avila said to Savage, voice cracking. It reminded Savage of a little girl losing her Barbie.

Burns pulled Avila away. Savage was glad. Some of Avila's pomade had dripped on his eyebrow.

"What's the matter with you, kid?" Burns said to Avila. "You want to get kicked off the force?"

"I ain't gonna listen to this five-time loser badmouth my

mom!"

"You got to be more of a man than that. He's just trying to goad you. C'mon, take a walk."

Avila huffed away. "This ain't over!" he said over his shoulder.

Police activity swallowed up the sight of Avila. Burns turned to Savage and scowled. He then walked towards the forensic van.

Savage felt a bit of triumph that he won the confrontation with that pretty boy Avila. Showed him who's boss.

The buzz of the confrontation soon faded. Savage inserted a wad of Red Man chewing tobacco into his mouth and wandered around the crime scene. He walked past a Mercedes and a Lexus. Next to the Lexus was an open suitcase turned upside-down. Savage saw a couple kilos of cocaine. Nearby, the fingerprint specialist mentioned to the medical examiner that no money was lying around. Savage's ears perked up. If a drug deal went bad, shouldn't the money and the drugs still be here, since apparently everyone got shot? Mentally noting that information, Savage sauntered off to the side, towards a parked white van. The van needed a cleaning—badly. A few yards from the van were two dead Hispanics, each armed.

Savage froze.

He saw tire tracks, ones that were obviously not made by the white van. These tracks were fresh.

Then, Savage saw a brown turd on the ground. Human feces. Fresh. Immediately, Savage thought of Chase Kilbey and how his Camaro smelled—literally—like shit.

Not one to believe in coincidences, Savage's mind turned towards surveillance options.

CHAPTER 42

Nick sat in the backseat of the Camaro, the suitcase of money resting on his lap. He was numb. What was he thinking, taking the money? It was, in every sense of the phrase, blood money. Taking it was wrong, with a capital *W*.

Thoughts of the money departed Nick's mind, replaced by an image of Jose dying: Mucus running from Jose's nose, and a film of saliva stretching across his open mouth. Saliva bubbles forming and bursting as Jose fought to catch his last breath. Nick sniffed. Strange how sex creates an intense bond.

"We're here," Chase said.

The Camaro pulled into the Best Western Hotel parking lot on Roosevelt Boulevard in Northeast Philadelphia. Chase had checked in before the prom, so they circumvented the lobby. The four of them walked down the hall, side by side, taking up its width. Chase unlocked the door with the key card.

The room had two beds. Chase and Monique sat on one while Steve lay on the other. Nick placed the suitcase on the bureau and quickly moved away from it.

Chase got up.

"What are ya doing?" Nick asked from the window.

"Going to open it," Chase answered.

Nick looked away. He heard the clasps click open. Chase whistled. Nick looked up. He couldn't see inside the suitcase. A ray of light from the bureau lamp shined off the suitcase's left clasp, creating a glare; plus, Chase only held the lid up halfway. Nick shifted. The glare disappeared. Nick smelled the money, a mixture of sweat, ink and paper.

Chase lifted the lid all the way until it rested against the mirror. Nick couldn't believe how much money was packed in there. Most of it was in hundreds, though there were other denominations, such as ones, fives, tens, twenties and fifties; one batch consisted of 1,000-dollar bills. Each batch was held together by a black binding clip.

"Wow," Chase said, "look at all this money." He fanned through a stack of twenties. Half of them were marked with blood, the bottom bill the worst—a blotch of crimson masking Andrew Jackson's face.

"How much do you think is there?" Monique asked.

Chase flapped his lips. "I don't know. Steve?"

Steve cleared his throat. "Three, four million."

"None of us would have to work...ever," Chase said, as if in a trance.

"Fuck that!" Nick stormed across the room.

"Huh?" Chase said.

Nick snapped the wad of bills out of Chase's hands and threw them in the suitcase.

"Wha—" Chase said, "what are you doing?"

Nick slammed the suitcase shut, lugged it across the room and tossed it into the closet. "We ain't keeping that money."

"Why not?" Chase asked. "You said Jose gave it to you."

"I shouldn't have taken it. I don't know what I was thinking. I must've been in shock or something."

"But, dude—"

"Chase," Nick said, "we can't keep it. It's drug money. It's wrong."

"Oh, give me a break!"

Monique stepped into the bathroom, carrying her overnight bag. Chase folded his arms and sat on the bureau, where the suitcase had rested. Nick stood by the closet, as if on guard. And Steve still lay on the bed.

"I don't see what the big deal is," Chase said. "So what if it's drug money. You think the money your mom gives you is squeaky clean?"

"What's that supposed to mean?" Nick said.

"Your mom works at S-Mart, right?"

"Of course she does. You know that."

"S-Mart's known for selling clothes that are produced by sweatshop labor. That's why stuff's sold so cheap. And because

S-Mart isn't paying a decent wage to make the clothes, they have money to hire your mom as a cashier. Compared to the money Jose gave you, it's essentially the same thing."

"Get the hell out of here," Nick said.

Monique exited the bathroom. She no longer wore her prom dress. She sported a short-sleeve shirt with a decal (Wildwood, NJ) and sweatpants from her old school (Cardinal Dougherty). Her hair was pulled back into a diminutive ponytail. Not a trace of makeup caked her face.

"You know," Monique said, "we could give the money to charity, like a school or something. Maybe we could drop it off anonymously. Or even better, give each school in the city ten thousand—you know, spread it around."

Nick yawned. "I'm too exhausted to think about it. I'm going to bed. See youse all tomorrow."

Aware that he was being rude but not caring, Nick crawled into bed and curled into a ball, falling asleep quicker than the average length of a Suicidal Tendencies tune. Sleep was so deep, he had no nightmares—at least none he remembered—about the night's events.

CHAPTER 43

Monday morning. The start of another school/work week. For some, when the alarm went off, they sprang out of bed, more excited than Ed Grimly to start the week anew with fresh opportunities and adventures. For others, they glared at the alarm clock and whacked the snooze button like a disgruntled judge, depressed that the weekend was officially over and the next two-day siesta was an epic 110 hours away.

Chase and Nick—at least this week—belonged to the former group. It was 7 A.M. They sat in the school cafeteria. They were the only ones here, besides the janitor, who was across the room, out of earshot, mopping the floor in front of the kitchen's closed aluminum counter shudders. Students wouldn't start trickling in for another half-hour.

"I can't believe you're still being a wet blanket about the money," Chase whispered.

"Can't help it," Nick whispered back, "it's the way I was raised."

"Dude, be serious."

"Be serious? How's this: I can't believe you kept that freakin' suitcase in your car all weekend."

Chase waved a dismissive hand. "Ah, it's no big deal. The Camaro was hardly out of my sight."

"Is the suitcase in there now?"

Chase nodded, glancing around furtively.

"I think we should toss that suitcase in the river," Nick said.

"The river?" Chase tried not to stutter.

"Yeah, the Delaware River."

"Whoa, whoa, whoa," Chase said. "Hit the brakes and back up. Toss it in the river? What are you, nuts?"

"It's not right. That money comes from the wallets and purses of weak people at their most desperate hour."

"So?"

Johnny Ostentatious

"So," Nick said, "it's like...it's like old man McNally."

"What are you bringing that old drunk up for?"

"Remember that time we were coming back from the movies? I think it was during winter, our freshman year. McNally was lying in the alley at the bottom of the hill under the Johnson's back porch."

"No," Chase said, "I don't remember."

"It was a Saturday night. McNally was passed out, as usual. Anyway, there were these three junior-high dickheads going through McNally's pockets, looking for his wallet. You talked me into helping scare 'em off, then we carried McNally home. Later, I asked you why you wanted to help McNally out. Do you remember what you said?"

Chase shook his head.

"I still remember it word for word," Nick said. "I asked ya, 'Man, why do you give a shit about a waste-oid like old man McNally? He's obviously intent on killing himself with the bottle.' And you said, 'Nick, I know he doesn't deserve a second thought, let alone our help, but he's a human being, and even though he's an inebriated mess, he doesn't deserve to have three little thugs-in-training rifle through his pockets when he can't even defend himself. It's just not right.'

"Chase, when you said that, I was totally blown away. I mean, it was around the time I was starting to get into punk rock and you weren't, and I was worrying that my love for punk might be the start of us drifting apart. But when you said all that stuff about old man McNally, I was like—to myself—'Right on, this guy's the shit! I'm gonna be best friends with this cat till the day I die. Not only does he have his head screwed on right, but it's perfectly torqued.'"

"I don't get it," Chase said.

"Yeah, I know, that analogy is a bit of a stretch, but you know what I mean. If we divvy up the money between the four of us, we're no better than those three thugs-in-training. It all revolves around money. We can't be profiting from people who suffer from substance abuse."

"Wait a minute."

"What?" Nick said.

"We don't know if that money came from selling drugs. Jose was using it to *buy* drugs, but we have no way of knowing if it came from *selling* drugs."

"Give me a fucking break, Chase. Even if it didn't come from selling drugs, it had to come from some sort of other unethical, illegal means, like gambling, extortion or prostitution. Hell, I may be attracted to Jose and all, but he's still a criminal."

Chase picked up on Nick referring to the dead Jose in the present tense. He decided not to point it out. Instead, he said, "Okay, fine. The money's dirty. You made your point—practically belabored it—but come on, let's keep it."

"I can't," Nick said. "I'd never be able to live with myself. My conscience would never let me live it down."

Chase forced himself to laugh.

"Sorry," Nick said.

"Come on, Nick. Please go along with it. I can't take my share unless we all go in on it."

"Really?"

"Yeah," Chase said. "It wouldn't be right."

"You're starting to sound like me. Pretty soon you'll be making asinine analogies to validate your argument."

They smiled at each other.

"A million dollars, Nick. Just think of what you could do with that money. You're always talking about wanting to run your own record label. You could use the money as start-up capital and still have enough left over to play music without worrying about the rent."

Nick didn't reply. Monique approached the table.

CHAPTER 44

"Hi, guys," Monique said.

"What's up?" Nick said.

Monique dropped her school bag on the table and sat next to Chase. He looked good. He was wearing a navy-blue shirt, which complemented his cobalt eyes and brown hair.

"Hey, hon," Chase said.

Monique froze. Did Chase just call her *hon*? He did, didn't he? She beamed. She liked him calling her *hon*. Sure, it may have been premature in their relationship. After all, they had only gone out on one date—the prom. But she really liked him, so much so that she scooted her chair closer to his. He rested his arm on the top of her chair. She leaned back. His hand touched her shoulder. Monique felt safe. Secure.

Chase said to Monique, "I've been trying to talk Nick into taking his share from the suitcase."

"And?" Monique said.

"And he's being more stubborn than Marlon Brando on the set of *Apocalypse Now*."

"I see," Monique said.

Steve joined them. "Morning."

Chase, Monique and Nick greeted Steve back.

"Yesterday afternoon," Monique said, "I was thinking about the whole deal with the suitcase. It's strange. Chase, you really want to dig into it; Nick, you're adamantly opposed to it; Steve is indifferent; and I want to give it all away."

"I guess we could give it away," Chase said.

Monique paused, wondering if Chase was pulling the New Boyfriend Act. In her experience, when you started dating a boy, for the first few months he was more agreeable than a congressional lobbyist. Monique stopped herself. Was Chase her boyfriend? No, not yet but soon. She had a feeling the business with the suitcase was going to speed up their relationship, similar to how couples fall in love quicker when they're coworkers.

"Then again," Chase said, "I really could use my share for when I go out to L.A. one day."

"L.A.?" Monique said.

"Yeah, I'd like to try and see if I can break into the acting scene out there."

"Hmm."

"That's all well and good," Nick said, "but it still looks like we're at a stalemate with this whole thing."

"Not really," Monique said. "While I was thinking about the suitcase over the weekend, I thought of something we could do with it."

"What's that?" Chase asked.

"Hide it."

"I like the way you think, Flemming," Nick said.

"Hide it?" Chase asked. "For how long?"

Monique shrugged. "Maybe until graduation. Hopefully by then we'll all be on the same page on what to do with it."

"I don't know," Chase said.

"I like it." Nick smirked. "It's smart, sensible and proactive."

"But where we going to stick it?" Chase asked.

That silenced the table. It was so quiet, you could hear a plastic fork drop.

At that point, students began entering the cafeteria. None sat near Monique, Chase, Nick and Steve. Nonetheless, the three of them lowered their voices (Steve didn't count because he kept quiet).

"Maybe," Nick said, "maybe we can hide it in a field, like how the guy did in that Stephen King story, 'Rita Hayworth and the Shawshank Redemption.'"

"I don't think that'll work," Chase said. "We'd have to drive all the way out to the suburbs, and there's a good chance the suitcase wouldn't be there when we got back."

"That's true," Nick said. "There's so much urban sprawl around here, even the 'burbs are beginning to look citified."

"How about an old, abandoned factory?" Monique suggested.

141

Nick snapped his fingers in Chase's face. "Your dad's place!"

"I don't know," Chase said. "I don't want to get him involved in this."

"It's perfect," Nick said, "right, Steve?"

Steve appeared to be daydreaming. Monique wondered what about. At the sound of his name, he whipped to attention, nodding.

Nick said to Chase, "Didn't you say there's a long-ass tunnel at your dad's work that you and your brother used to explore?"

"Yeah, but—"

"It's perfect. Let's do it next weekend."

"Hold on," Chase said. "This isn't going to work."

"How do you mean?" Monique asked.

"What am I supposed to do, rap on the front gate and say, 'Hey, Dad, do you mind if me and my friends stash this suitcase in here?' 'Why's that, son?' 'Well, seems we can't make up our mind on what to do with it. It's only temporarily, until we graduate next June.' 'Is that all? Sure, come on in.'"

"We don't tell him," Nick said. "We sneak it in."

"What if we get caught?" Chase asked.

"We won't get caught."

The preliminary homeroom bell rang. Monique glanced at her Casio watch. It was 7:45 A.M. Time flies when you're fretting over four million dollars.

CHAPTER 45

Bruno Savage watched Kilbey and his three friends trot up the stairs to class. Savage was standing in the middle of the cafeteria, next to one of the square, lime-green pillars.

"Hey! Hey, you!" said a man with a Polish accent.

Savage diverted his attention from the Kilbey perp to the Polack.

The Polack was relatively short, had a hump as if an osteoporosis sufferer, was bald except for white tufts above his ears, and wore dentures that wouldn't stay in place.

"Hey, you," the Polack said again, "what do you think you're doing?"

"Holding this pillar up," Savage said humorlessly.

"What— You…"

"Spit it out, old man."

"You," the Polack said, "you… What are you doing wearing my uniform? W—Why do you have my mop?"

Savage looked down. He forgot he had broken into the janitor's closet and *acquired* the aforementioned items.

"Oh, I'm sorry," Savage said. "I must've been sleepwalking again."

Savage handed over the mop and bucket, then undid the uniform. It was the type that zippered down the front.

Savage stepped out of the uniform. His face abruptly took on a demonic edge. He threw the uniform over the Polack and pulled it tight. The Polack gasped, mouth open, sucking in and out on one of the uniform's hip pockets. Savage put the Polack in a headlock. The Polack dropped the mop, its wooden handle clacking on the floor.

"Try and give me shit, you little fuckin' cunt," Savage muttered.

Savage forced the Polack's left leg into the bucket. Black mop water splashed on Savage's polyester pants. He punched the

Polack in the stomach. The Polack doubled over. Savage pushed him away. The Polack wheeled towards the pillar that Savage had been lounging next to. The Polack banged into the pillar and fell down. The bucket tipped over. Mop water streamed across the cafeteria floor, towards the boys bathroom. A couple students stood up from a table in the corner. It didn't escape Savage that they were large for their age. They both wore varsity football jackets. *Must be linebackers.*

Savage strode for the door. He purposefully moved halfway between a run and a walk. Outside, he cut through the smokers' area and hopped the wrought iron fence. On the sidewalk, he ambled. Nobody was pursuing him, and he wasn't worried about any cafeteria kids IDing him. Things had happened too fast. Besides, he had kept his head low, so his face was unrecognizable.

At the end of the block, parked in front of a fire hydrant, was Savage's Plymouth. He slid in and pulled away. At the first red light, he removed a handheld tape recorder from his pocket and rewound it. The traffic light turned green. Savage pressed the recorder's play button. He listened to the conversation between Kilbey and his friends. The recording was less than optimal. Savage needed a stronger microphone. The minute mike he had placed on the tip of the mop handle only picked up one out of every five words. (Savage had pocketed the mike before the Polack confronted him.) Savage kept rewinding the tape to the part where Kilbey and Marsh mentioned where the money was currently stashed. Couldn't make it out. Savage pulled over. He rewound the tape one more time. Nope. Still too inaudible.

"Fuckin'," Savage said.

Savage squeezed the tape recorder in his hand until he was shaking. He eventually started to scream like a street fighter cranked up on adrenaline. He slammed the recorder on the dashboard again and again and again until the useless recorder was nothing more than shards of plastic and electronics.

Savage placed his hands on his lap. The hand that smashed the recorder was bleeding at the knuckles. Savage didn't care. He slurped on the blood and looked up. A mother stared at him. She had a baby in a stroller and a chubby-faced five-year-old boy at her side, clinging to her ankle-length flowery dress. Savage's eyes met the mother's. She did a 180 and chugged down the street, disappearing around the corner quicker than you could say *domestic threat*.

Savage couldn't care less. He finished slurping on his knuckles, then coasted his Plymouth down the street.

CHAPTER 46

On Wednesday, Nick was at Chinaski's Salvage Yard. Nick practiced here on Tuesdays, Thursdays and Saturdays with his punk band, Jesus Christ On Roller Skates, but he frequently stopped by on the remaining days of the week to hang out with Henry Chinaski, the owner of the yard.
   Mr. Chinaski was a unique individual. He was sixty years old. But that didn't make him unique. What did was his love for punk rock. How many sixty-year-olds do you know who like—let alone love—punk?
   Mr. Chinaski's office, located in the middle of the yard, was packed with punk-rock records, mostly The Ramones. Mr. Chinaski loved The Ramones almost as much as he loved Old Grand Dad whisky. Mr. Chinaski owned everything the Blitzkrieg Bop boys put out, even imports with bonus tracks that didn't appear on any of their domestic releases.
   Nick often wondered if Mr. Chinaski was into punk because he was a beatnik back in the fifties. Nick enjoyed listening to Mr. Chinaski tell stories from the days when he lived in Greenwich Village. One story Mr. Chinaski loved to tell was when he and Allen Ginsberg went over to William Burroughs' apartment unannounced around lunchtime. Jack Kerouac was passed out on the living-room floor with whiskey bottles surrounding him like numbers on a clock, and Burroughs was at the kitchen table, slumped over with a heroin needle sticking out of his arm. Mr. Chinaski decided to have a little fun. He told Ginsberg his idea for a practical joke, and the poet was, in Mr. Chinaski's words, "being a bit of a wet blanket, which didn't surprise me—he was always a bit of a pussy in those days." But after some cajoling, Ginsberg agreed to be Mr. Chinaski's partner in practical joking. They dragged Burroughs and Kerouac into the bedroom and stripped them naked. Ginsberg and Mr. Chinaski didn't stick around for when Burroughs and Kerouac woke up, and the

writers of their generation never mentioned the incident, either privately or in the press. Mr. Chinaski tried luring them once, saying how he had great respect for out-of-the-closet homosexuals; they were brave and definitive society misfits. But Burroughs and Kerouac never bit the bait. "I don't know why they never brought it up," Mr. Chinaski would say, ending the story. "I'm assuming Jack, who—unlike Will—was ashamed of his homosexuality, woke up first and hightailed it out of there. We'll never really know. One of life's little mysteries, I guess…"

But Nick didn't get to hear any of Mr. Chinaski's stories today. The sixteen-year-old only hung out with the recovering beatnik for a couple minutes. Nick was meeting his friends near the yard's front gate at four o'clock.

Nick reached the front gate a little after four. Chase, Monique and Steve were already waiting for him. Nick guided them through aisles of old car and truck parts, glass crackling underneath their feet. They stopped near the car crusher.

"Youse ready?" Nick asked.

Chase, Monique and Steve nodded.

"Okay," Nick said, "let's get started."

Chase began with how he thought they should stash the suitcase at the plant his father worked at. Nick offered some suggestions, and Monique revised the plan in an attempt to make it flawless. Steve contributed nothing to the discussion. He was told what to do.

"Is that a wrap?" Chase asked. "We cool?"

"Cooler than Johnny Rotten at the dentist," Nick said, leading them out of the salvage yard.

CHAPTER 47

Bruno Savage stood on a railroad bridge. Under the bridge was Comly Street, where trash covered the sidewalks. Local residents tossed their undesirables there when the trash men wouldn't pick up refuse they deemed too bulky. Common trash that littered the sidewalks under the bridge were furniture, car parts, eight-tracks and Beta videotapes. Residents dumped their rubbish here because you needed a car to go to the city dump, and most residents didn't drive due to Philadelphia's astronomical insurance rates.

On the bridge, Savage stood to the side of the train tracks. Altogether, there were four pairs of tracks. The inner tracks were for Amtrak, the outer tracks for South Eastern Transportation Authority's high-speed commuter trains.

Savage lifted his left foot and rested it on the bridge's iron ledge; his steel-tip toe tapped the head of a big bolt, which SEPTA had painted silver grey, like the rest of the bridge. Savage's right foot remained on the ground replete with granite rocks.

At 4:30 P.M., a SEPTA train flew by on the tracks closest to Savage. The conductor honked the horn as if experiencing railroad rage. Savage didn't move. His trench coat flapped like the cape of a comic-book villain.

"What are you fuckin' kids up to?" Savage muttered. He was peering through his binoculars at Chase Kilbey, Monique Flemming, Nick Marsh and Steve Atkinson. They were exiting Chinaski's Salvage Yard. Kilbey and Flemming, lollygagging in step, had their arms wrapped around each other. *Fools*, Savage thought. *Were they really so naïve to think their infatuation would* blossom *into love? Idiots.*

Savage placed Charlie into his trench coat pocket. "Charlie" was what he called his binoculars. He and Charlie had gone through some good times together. Charlie was a good-luck charm if there ever was any. Charlie had been with Savage since his days in Vietnam, back when he was the best sniper in the army.

Savage left the bridge, walking down a dirt hill to Comly Street, where he had parked his Plymouth. He wondered what Kilbey and his friends were up to. He'd find out, though. After the fiasco Monday morning in the cafeteria, Savage had planted a bug under Kilbey's dashboard.

Reaching his car, Savage criticized himself for the attention he caused by beating up that Polack. That was careless. If he wanted to go to extremes like that, he could kidnap Kilbey and torture him until he confessed to where the money was. But that would have been a dumb maneuver because after finding out the location of the money, Savage would have to kill Kilbey. Savage was a lot of things, but he wasn't a murderer.

Starting the Plymouth, Savage was grateful that nobody at the precinct suspected money from the crime scene was MIA. The last thing Savage needed was competition.

CHAPTER 48

On Friday, like every other weekday afternoon, Chase was driving Nick home from school. Chase pulled up in front of the Marsh house. Nick opened the car door, schoolbag on lap, and paused with one foot on the street.

"Tomorrow's the big day," Nick said.

"Yeah," Chase said. "You ready?"

Nick nodded.

"Okay," Chase said, "I'll see you tomorrow then."

"It's just..." Nick sucked on his lower lip. "Have you noticed anything strange about Steve lately?"

"How do you mean?"

"He seems lackadaisical about the whole thing, you know? I mean, me, you and Monique all have strong feelings about the money, but Steve doesn't seem to care. That just seems kinda weird. It's almost like he's a robot or something—no feelings whatsoever."

"Ah," Chase said, "he's a good kid. He's probably just overwhelmed by the whole thing."

"It doesn't strike you as strange that he seems so detached from it all, like he's a human computer analyzing the situation for some algorithm?"

"I wouldn't worry about it. Steve's Steve. He's a little short on social skills, but that doesn't mean he isn't a good person. Besides, we need him."

"Yeah, I know," Nick said, getting out of the Camaro. He closed the door, then spoke through the open window. "See ya tomorrow morning."

"Wouldn't miss it for the world."

CHAPTER 49

Standing outside the plant his father worked at, Chase formed a fist, relaxed it, then inhaled deeply through his nose. He spoke over his shoulder to Monique, Nick and Steve. "Ready?"

Monique said, "Mm-hmm." Steve nodded. And Nick, wearing Ray-Ban sunglasses, said, "Let's do it."

Chase took a step closer to the front gate. It was three o'clock on a hot, bright Saturday afternoon. The sun shined on the gate's intercom button. Chase pressed the red button and released it. A minute later, a voice crackled through static:

"Yeah."

"Chase Kilbey for Russell Kilbey."

"Hold on."

Chase dropped his hands in front of him, one hand over the other, similar to the way actors pose during photo shoots for publicity stills of a mobster movie. Chase glanced at his Timex watch. He wished his dad would hurry up. He was sweating more than Nell Carter under floodlights. Of course, it didn't help that he, like Nick and Steve, wore long baggy pants.

Chase's father strode across the yard. Chase drew on every iota of his acting ability and pretended he was Indiana Jones. Cool, calm and collected.

"What's up, Dad?"

"Same old, same old," Mr. Kilbey replied. "Ready for the big tour?"

CHAPTER 50

Standing in the plant yard, Monique wondered if Chase had been adopted. He shared no physical characteristics with his father. Mr. Kilbey was a short, stocky man with olive-colored skin, although, his eyes did glint when he smiled, just like Chase's.

"What class is this for again?" Mr. Kilbey asked.

"It's for our Social Studies class," Chase said. "We're supposed to research and write about something industrial."

"Ah-hah," Mr. Kilbey said. "Let me throw this paperwork in the office real quick, then I'll give you the penny tour."

"You're not too busy today, are you?" Chase asked.

"Nah, we run with a skeleton crew on Saturdays, with a light workload. You know that."

"Oh, that's right."

"Wait here," Mr. Kilbey said.

Monique and the boys—as she was beginning to call them—stood in the yard, halfway between the front gate and the plant's main building. Mr. Kilbey ran into a trailer, which Monique assumed was his office. He popped out twenty seconds later.

The five of them entered the main building. Mr. Kilbey led Monique and the boys down a long, wide walkway. On the right were tin walls with intermittent corridors; Monique guessed offices or meeting rooms lied down there. On the left were heavy-duty machines and conveyor belts, currently inactive. That side smelled of oil and copper.

"Nothing much to see here," Mr. Kilbey said, motioning to the left. "That equipment's out-of-date. We're breaking it down for parts."

Monique felt Chase tug her arm. His chin pointed down a corridor to the right. So that's where they were going to hide the money.

Peripherally, Monique saw Chase tap Steve's elbow. Steve reached in his pocket and pressed the button to a gadget that announced on the cone-shaped speaker overhead: "PAGING RUSSELL KILBEY. PLEASE REPORT TO THE DIXON BUILDING."

"What!" Mr. Kilbey said. "Of all the times..." The Dixon Building was at the other end of the plant. Mr. Kilbey closed his eyes and touched the bridge of his nose. He opened his eyes. "This might take awhile. Youse want to wait in my office till I get back? There's a TV and radio in there."

"Sure," Chase said.

Mr. Kilbey jogged away.

Chase smiled at Steve. "It worked."

Mr. Kilbey stopped jogging. "Chase!"

Monique watched Chase tense up and remove his smile before turning around to face his father, who stood one hundred yards away.

"Yeah?" Chase said.

"There's some Tastykakes in my top-left drawer, if you and your friends want any. They're krimpets."

"Okay."

Mr. Kilbey resumed his jog. He turned down a corridor and was gone.

"Way to go, Steve," Chase said, patting him on the back.

On Wednesday, at the salvage yard, Chase had proposed they drop by the plant unannounced, ask his father for a quick tour and hope he got called away. Nick suggested they not arrive unannounced, and Monique recommended that once they were at the plant, they should make Mr. Kilbey get called away. Could Steve come up with something? Steve said he would try, and he came through. He had created a palm-size gadget with a red button in the center. When you pressed the button and aimed it at a speaker, the message paging Mr. Kilbey came out. On Thursday at lunch, in a rare moment of loquacity, Steve excitedly explained how the gadget worked, which Monique failed to understand. Math and science were her academic strong points, but the technology Steve used for the gadget was beyond her education. Maybe after graduate school she would understand the science behind it, but not at age seventeen. Was Steve a genius? After all, he'd constructed the gadget in three days—in his spare time.

"Come on," Chase said, "we don't have much time. Once he gets down there and realizes he's been duped, he'll be back in a flash."

"How much time we got?" Nick asked.

"Gee, I don't know. Let's see..."

"All right. You said it's a ten-minute walk to the Dixon Building, right?"

"Right."

"Okay," Nick said, "so he'll probably run all the way down there. That'll take about five minutes. Once he gets there, he'll walk around for five or ten minutes, looking around for who paged him, then he'll walk back—another five, ten minutes. So we got twenty, twenty-five minutes. Half-hour at the very most. What time is it now?"

Chase looked at his Timex. "3:20."

"We should try and make it back by 3:35—3:50 at the latest."

"Actually," Monique said, "you better make it a quarter to four. You just wasted five minutes standing around talking about it. Honestly, guys, you should've discussed this earlier."

"You're right," Nick said.

"Let's go!" Chase said, darting for the corridor.

CHAPTER 51

Nick followed Chase down the corridor; Steve brought up the rear. Monique stayed behind to act as lookout.

On Wednesday, Nick and Monique talked about who should be the lookout. Chase didn't participate in the discussion because he was the only one who knew where to hide the money. Nick felt he should go, too, since he was in good athletic shape. So it was between Steve and Monique. Nick urged Monique to be the lookout. She agreed. Nick was glad it didn't take too much persuasion. He hadn't said it, but he thought if Mr. Kilbey came back earlier than expected, Monique would handle it better than Steve, who would stammer and blush more than Jimmy Stewart.

Nick, Chase and Steve continued running down the corridor. The tin walls on either side merged into slate walls. Nick noticed the ceiling was lower than when they started their run. Fluorescent lights hung from the ten-foot-high ceiling. Half of the fluorescent bulbs either flickered or were burned out. The lights that did work illuminated the rain cracks on the slate walls. But that didn't last long. The farther Nick and his two friends ran down the corridor, the dimmer the lights became until it was pitch dark. Prepared for this eventuality, the three of them pulled out headlamps from their pockets; the headlamps consisted of compact flashlights attached to leather headbands. They put the headlamps on. Since Nick, Chase and Steve were still running, the light beams bounced off the slate floors, walls and ceilings. Despite this, Nick made out the pipes running along the corners of the ceiling. Insulation around the pipes was yellow from old age. Cracks in it had been sealed with red, black and white stickers. WARNING: ASBESTOS.

Nick pulled his shirt over his mouth and nose. "Fuckin' A! What the hell is that?"

"Oh," Chase said, "the waste from the plant runs down these pipes here." Still running, he pointed at the pipes bracketed from the ceiling corners that Nick had previously noticed. "They dump the waste into some huge vat," Chase finished.

The stench grew stronger. To Nick, it smelled like feces dipped in sour milk, then locked in a room on a hot day.

They reached the vat. Its circumference of ten feet almost blocked their path. Nick and his two cohorts squeezed around it. No waste gushed into it now, however, some waste did drip from the pipes that elbowed off the ceiling and pointed down towards the vat. The waste was brownish-green.

On the other side of the vat was the mouth of a cave. Nick and Steve followed Chase. Several steps into the cave, Nick saw bats hanging from the ceiling. Steve gasped.

"Don't worry," Chase said. "They're harmless."

"D—d—do—do they ever fly into the plant?" Steve asked.

"No, they go in the other direction, out to the sewer. It leads up to the street gutter."

They went a few feet past the bats, when Chase announced, "We're here."

Nick removed his headlamp, then pulled off his shirt. Chase and Steve did the same. Taped to their torsos was the money in large Ziploc sandwich bags. They threw the money on the ground. The Ziploc plastic smelled of teenage sweat, which nauseated Nick, even though a third of it was his.

Next, Nick and his friends dropped their pants to tear off more Ziploc bags masking-taped to their legs. They had taped them so only a few hairs suffered the fate of being yanked out by the roots.

A few minutes later, Nick, Chase and Steve were fully dressed, headlamps back on. In front of them sat the pile of four million dollars. Chase stepped over the cash.

"Give me a hand, will you?" he said.

Nick helped Chase move aside a medium-size rock. It was heavier than it looked. Nick exerted himself so much, he felt his stomach and groin muscles tighten.

After rolling the rock aside, Nick scratched his head. The hole in the wall wasn't that large—barely big enough for a cub to curl up and hibernate in.

"You sure all the money'll fit in there?" Nick asked.

Chase nodded.

Leaving the money in the Ziploc bags, they packed it into the hole. It fit, barely. Chase and Nick rolled the rock back. They turned to leave. Chase stopped, glancing back at the rock. Nick knew what his best friend was doing. Making sure the placement of the rock looked natural. It did.

"What time is it?" Nick asked.

Chase brought his Timex to his face, lighted by his headlamp. "Quarter to four."

"Holy shit, we gotta get back!"

They sprinted down the corridor.

CHAPTER 52

Monique looked at her watch. What was taking them so long? She crossed her arms and leaned against the pillar with the speaker that over a half-hour ago had paged Mr. Kilbey to the Dixon Building.

Uh-oh.

Monique watched a man approach. She had hoped this wouldn't happen. So what if the plant operated with a skeleton crew on weekends? Why couldn't one of the workers show up when they first arrived, or wait until Chase got back from the corridor?

The worker strutted closer. He wore faded blue jeans, a black ZZ Top T-shirt and a Phillies baseball cap.

"Hey, little darling," he said in a raspy voice Monique identified with a steady diet of cigars and hard liquor.

"Hi," Monique said, arms still folded across her chest.

"What's a pretty little thing like you doing in a place like this?"

"Waiting for Russell Kilbey to come back and finish giving us the tour."

"Kilbey, huh?"

Monique nodded. The man leered.

Not knowing what to say or do, Monique went with: "So, is Mr. Kilbey your boss?"

The man laughed as if hearing an off-color joke. His head bent back and he roared. Monique noted his scruffy beard. It was more unattractive on the underside than on his cheeks.

The man dropped his chin and smiled. His left incisor was black-green.

"Let me tell you something, little darling." He hooked his thumbs under his Hee-Haw belt buckle. "Ronald Warzinski is his own man. Kilbey may be the foreman around here, but he don't tell me what to do. You follow me?"

Monique nodded. Timidly.

"You know," the man said, "I don't have to work here. I could get up, clear out my locker and get another job"—he snapped his fingers—"like that."

Monique knew she should keep quiet and let the *conversation* die, letting this character creep away so he could crawl back under the heavy-metal rock he came from, but she couldn't resist asking: "Why don't you?"

"Why don't I what?"

"Get another job."

"Why should I?" he said, indignant. "I work hard for my money. If they wanna get rid of me, they'll have to fire me. Then you know what I'll do? I'll take 'em to court and sue 'em for all they're worth." He grinned.

"I see."

"Nobody tells Ronald Warzinski how to live his life, not even the ladies."

Once again, Monique nodded. She prayed this character would depart soon. She couldn't take much more of his ignorance.

"So, honey," he said, "I'm going square-dancing next weekend. Care to come?"

Monique went rigid.

CHAPTER 53

Chase stopped. Nick and Steve ran into him from behind.

"What the—" Nick said.

"Shh," Chase said, pointing. A worker was talking to Monique. Chase, Nick and Steve were in the corridor, fifty yards away. "What should we do?" Chase whispered.

"Let's wait," Nick whispered back.

The worker said to Monique, "What, you think you're too good to go out with me?"

"No, I'm involved with someone."

"You're lying!" the worker said.

Monique sighed.

Chase felt Nick tap him on the elbow. "Come on," the punk rocker said.

Chase, Nick and Steve stepped out of the corridor.

"Hey, hon," Chase said, wrapping an arm around Monique's shoulders, "what's going on?"

"Nothing much," Monique said. "I was just talking to Mr. Warzinski."

At that moment, Mr. Kilbey approached. "I thought you and your friends were going to wait in my office."

Chase played evasive by asking, "How did it go over in—what was it?—the Dixon Building?"

"It was the weirdest thing," Mr. Kilbey said. "Nobody was over there. Doesn't look like anybody's been over there all day." He stared at Warzinski. "It's almost as if paging me was a practical joke."

"What're you looking at me like that for?" Warzinski exclaimed.

"Where were you a half-hour ago?" Mr. Kilbey asked.

"I was taking my lunch."

"In the break room?"

"Yeah, but—" Warzinski said.

"Which would put you in vicinity of the paging mike."

"But I didn't do it, I swear!"

"In my office now, Warzinski," Mr. Kilbey said.

Warzinski stomped away.

"Come on," Mr. Kilbey said to Chase and his friends, "I'll see you out."

CHAPTER 54

Bruno Savage parked his Plymouth down the street from Taylor Manufacturing. He whipped out Charlie, his binoculars, to see Kilbey and his cohorts getting into the Camaro. They must have already stashed the money in the plant. *Damn!* Savage wished he had gotten here when they first arrived; then he could have worn a ski mask and robbed them. But no, he had to stay late at the precinct filling out paperwork. Stupid bureaucrats and their endless miles of red tape.

The Camaro pulled away. Savage didn't tail them. Why bother? He knew the money was in the plant. The other day, Kilbey mentioned it (code word: suitcase—*how obvious*) to Marsh while they were driving home from school. The bug that Savage had Crazy-Glued under the Camaro dash was working just fine.

The Plymouth's passenger door swung open. In slid Tim Burns. Savage jumped. He jumped again when he looked in front of his car. There stood Richie Avila, the rookie he harassed for a hobby. Avila rested a foot on the front bumper.

"How's it going, Bruno?" Burns said.

"Okay till you got here."

"So Richie and I are at the station, chugging down some java, talking about last night's game, when what do we see? You tearing out of the station like Bruce Jenner."

Savage, staring at the steering wheel, traced the Plymouth emblem with his index finger.

"What are you up to, Bruno?"

"None of your business," Savage said.

"With an answer like that," Burns said, "why do I get the feeling you're guiltier than Ted Bundy?"

Savage didn't reply.

Burns got out of the Plymouth. He slammed the passenger door, then bent over. "Richie and I are watching you. You give cops a bad name, Bruno. Most of us are out there busting our humps to make this godforsaken city a better place—for practically minimum wage, I might add—and you're out there acting like a con. You're a sly one, Bruno, I'll give you that, but your luck is about to run out. Just ask Traci Miller."

Savage met Burns' gaze. "Who?"

"You know who she is," Burns said. "She's been talking to Internal Affairs. Looks like they're starting a file on you. I can't wait for the trial. Richie and I will be more than happy to testify. See you around, Dee-tective."

Burns swiped Charlie from the dashboard and left. Savage didn't make a move to retrieve his binoculars because he wanted to appear nonchalant over Burns' threats.

Avila and Burns strutted down the street. Before turning the corner, Avila, frowning, glanced back and shook his head.

When they were finally gone, Savage brought a hand to his face. He was shaking worse than a multiple sclerosis sufferer. "Holy fuck," he mumbled into his palm.

Going to have to play the good son for awhile. Or at least until the heat dies down.

1984

CHAPTER 55

Nick stood in Chase's backyard. It was the middle of June, a little after midnight. The graduation party was winding down.

Nick leaned against an elm tree. The night was fairly humid, although a warm breeze cut through the yard occasionally. Gnats, mosquitoes and fireflies danced around Nick's head. He swatted the gnats and mosquitoes away but didn't bother the fireflies.

"There you are," Chase said, striding across the yard, the grass muffling the sound of his flip-flops. "What are you doing?"

"Taking a moment to reflect," Nick said, smirking.

"Yeah, it has been a pretty hectic day, hasn't it?" Chase said seriously.

"Chase?" said a voice from the back door. Monique.

"Over here," Chase said.

Monique joined her boyfriend and the punk rocker. "What are you doing?" she asked.

"Getting away for a couple minutes," Chase said. "Hey, have you seen Steve?"

"He's in the basement playing Space Invaders with your brother," Monique said.

"Let me go get him real quick. There's something I want to talk with you all about." Chase ran for the house.

"Looks like we're going to have a meeting of the minds," Nick said.

"I wonder what about," Monique said.

"Three guesses, the first four don't count," Nick said, walking to the patio to retrieve a small plastic table, four plastic chairs, and an insect repellent candle. After setting down the table and chairs in front of Monique and the elm tree, Nick lit the candle with his lighter. The candle glowed orange and seemed to do a better job of attracting gnats and mosquitoes than repelling them.

Chase returned with Steve. All four sat down.

"Check it out," Nick said with an impish glint in his eyes, "teenagers of the patio table."

"Very nice," Chase said. "Okay, since we're all here, I thought we'd talk about the suitcase." It had been thirteen months since they'd hidden the four million dollars in the plant. "What do you all want to do with it?"

"Leave it," Nick said.

"Leave it?"

"Leave it."

"But," Chase stammered, "but what if something happens to it?"

"So what if it does? It's dirty. Let it sit there and rot for all I care."

"There's another option," Monique said.

"What's that?" Nick asked.

"We can treat it like insurance."

"Huh?" Chase said.

"We're all eighteen years old, right?" Monique began. "We just graduated from high school with our whole lives ahead of us. Let's leave it there for—say—twenty years. We come back then, and meet and decide what to do with it."

"I like it," Nick said, smiling. "It's smart, sensible, and proactive."

"But something can happen to it by then," Chase said. "The plant could blow up, or somebody could stumble across it."

"I don't think we have anything to worry about," Monique said. "From the way you described it, it sounds like it's in a pretty safe place."

"I don't know, hon," Chase said.

Monique placed a hand on Chase's arm. "It'll be fine," she said. "I'm sure by the millennium, you'll be a big, famous actor, and you won't care about the suitcase."

"Yeah," Nick said, "and I'll be sticking it to the system in one form or another. And Steve—well, who knows what the fuck you'll be doing."

Steve didn't reply.

"Okay," Nick said, "so that's it. We all get together in 2004 and see where we are with our stations in life."

"Whoa," Chase said, "2004! It's already been sitting there a year."

"Jesus Christ. Okay, okay. We'll do it in 2003. Happy?"

"I'd rather go and get it now, but, yeah, I'll wait."

"Cool," Nick said, "now if youse'll all excuse me, I need to go home and get some beauty sleep."

"Later."

Back to the Future

CHAPTER 56

Tomorrow was the big day. Time to retrieve the four million dollars. Nick had to admit, he was more than a little excited. With his share, he would never have to hold another day job again. Of course, it helped that he hovered a few pennies above poverty level.

Nick clapped his hands and rubbed his palms together, then picked up his bass. He was sitting in Chase and Monique's Astro Van. It was 10:00 P.M. The van was parked in front of Mr. Flemming's house. Mr. Flemming didn't want Spanky the harp seal in his house (he had half-joked, "That seal's skin is slimier than my ex-wife's personality"), so Nick, still homeless, had volunteered to stay in the van and seal-sit Spanky. Monique had thanked Nick and lent him a key to the house, in case he wanted to crawl into the living room and crash on the couch. He kept the key in his bass-guitar case but didn't think he'd take Monique up on her offer. He didn't mind sleeping in the van. Hell, he'd been sleeping in vans most of his adult life. Ahhh, the glamorous life of being in a touring punk-rock band.

Nick played his bass for the next half-hour. He worked on the bass lines of a song he was writing. He was having some trouble with the break—couldn't seem to get it right. He knew why. Usually when songwriting, he chain-smoked like a brass monkey. He didn't now because Spanky was in the van. Secondhand smoke kills.

Unable to concentrate, Nick placed his bass in its leather case and said to Spanky, "I don't know, I just don't know. Know what I'm saying, dawg?"

Spanky perked up in the back of the van, where he'd been dozing. He scooted up to Nick and rested his head on the punk rocker's lap. Nick jerked at first, then warmed up to the seal. He petted Spanky's noggin. The seal's left flipper twitched. A sign of pleasure, Nick assumed.

Soon, Spanky fell asleep in Nick's lap. He continued to pet the seal, albeit absently. He was recalling the night of his junior prom. He wondered what would have happened if Jose hadn't been gunned down. Would they have become an item? Would they still be together today? Who knows.

Nick tapped Spanky on the nose. The seal stirred awake. Nick stretched out on an exercise mat that Monique had brought out earlier. He tucked a rolled-up T-shirt underneath his head and fell asleep, Spanky snoozing at his side.

CHAPTER 57

Meanwhile, inside the Flemming household, Monique showered and shaved, then retired to her bedroom, the same one she grew up in. The bed from her youth was long gone. Years ago, her father had given it away to the Salvation Army and bought a queen-size bed from Diamond Furniture. That way, whenever she and Chase visited, they'd have something comfortable to sleep on.

Chase was in bed already. He was sitting up, on top of the covers, his back against the headboard, hands behind his head. He gazed up at a corner of the ceiling.

"What are you thinking about?" Monique asked from the foot of the bed.

"Tomorrow," Chase answered.

"Anything specifically?"

Chase shook his head. "Just how it will go off."

"I'm sure it'll be fine," Monique said, dressing for bed.

"Yeah, you're probably right."

Monique lay next to Chase, placing her head on his chest and resting her hand on his thigh.

"When I was in the shower," Monique said, "I was thinking about how much things have changed."

"Like how Nick now wants the money?"

"That and how Steve is basically a different person."

"Yeah," Chase said, "he sure has done well for himself."

"You don't think—this is a horrible thing to say—you don't think he ever snuck into the plant and stole the money, do you?"

"Steve? No way. I know today he's an aggressive businessman and everything, but I think he does it with a little bit of class, you know?"

Monique shrugged. "I don't know. He never did say where he got the money to start that computer company of his. Remember?"

Chase nodded.

Back in 1995, Steve had stopped by Monique and Chase's apartment in California. (Steve was in town for a computer convention.) By that point, Steve had been a millionaire for several years. Coincidentally, Monique and Chase were having trouble meeting their bills that year. In five months, Chase had only one paying acting job; and that year, Monique didn't receive a raise at the zoo due to budget cuts. So, after dinner, Chase asked Steve for a little loan—a thousand dollars or two. Steve said he would lend them the money, but at thirty-percent interest, compounded daily. When Monique heard that, she almost dropped the glass she was washing in the sink. Here was one of the richest people in the country sitting in their kitchen, and he had the audacity to act like a loan shark. Steve justified his position by saying he wasn't fond of "giving handouts." He believed people should work for their money. Monique couldn't believe what she was hearing. Shaking her head, she finished washing the dishes and didn't say anything until Steve left. Then she went off. She couldn't believe how greedy Steve was—never mind he had sidestepped the casual question during dinner of where he obtained the capital to start his computer company. Chase tried defending Steve, but Monique cut him off. It wasn't like they met him *after* he became rich. They had known him *since* high school. "Jeez, Chase," Monique said, "you took him under your wing when nobody else wanted anything to do with him. That has to count for something." Chase's reply was: "I don't know."

Snapping out of the flashback, Monique said to Chase, "I don't trust him, hon."

"Who? Steve?"

"Mm-hmmm."

"Come on," Chase said, "he isn't all that bad. I know nowadays he can seem a little rough around the edges, but he's basically the same guy we knew back in high school. He's all right."

Monique removed her head from Chase's chest. She touched

his after-shave-smelling cheek and said, "You have such a huge heart, always looking for the best in people. It's a weakness at times." She felt his body stiffen. "But it's also part of the reason why I love you so much." Chase relaxed.

"Only part, huh?" Chase said. "What's the other part?"

Monique raised a flirtatious eyebrow.

"Oh," Chase said.

Monique leaned in towards Chase, pulling the top sheet over them, both of them giggling.

CHAPTER 58

Across town, Bruno Savage sat in Pierce Price's Spyder. Down the street was the plant where Kilbey had hidden the money twenty years ago. Price wasn't here. He was keeping watch on the Flemming residence.

Savage got out of the Spyder to stretch his legs. The night was unusually cool for May. Despite the coolness, Savage smelled rain in the air. There had been no precipitation for at least a month, so it was a safe bet that it was going to rain.

Savage stood outside the plant. Inside, behind the fence, paced two dogs. A German shepherd and a Doberman pinscher.

Savage puffed on a cigarette. After he smoked it down to the filter, he flicked it into the yard. The Doberman's ears pricked up. It raced after the butt, disappearing into the darkness. But the German shepherd didn't chase the spent cigarette; it swaggered up to the gate and growled.

"Go fuck yourself," Savage said, pulling out another cigarette.

The German shepherd squeezed its snout between the dual gate. The bottom of the gate's chain grazed the top of the shepherd's head. The dog showed off its coffee-colored teeth.

The Doberman returned to the gate, tongue lolling out of its mouth. It tried to imitate the German shepherd by inserting its snout between the end of the gate and a fence post.

Bored with the dogs, Savage stepped away from the fence and returned to the Spyder. He didn't think Kilbey and the three musketeers were going to retrieve the money tonight. Price had informed Savage that Kilbey and his wife had turned in for the evening, as had Marsh in the van parked in front of the Flemming house, and Atkinson was at an Asian spa in Center City.

Savage slid into the Spyder, knocked the seat back and closed his eyes. He recalled being kicked off the force on October 25, 1995. It took 12 years for Internal Affairs to put a solid case against Savage, and unfortunately for him, Tim Burns was running IA. The case was so rock-solid that Savage's lawyer didn't even show up for the hearing. Savage found himself unemployed quicker than the cancellation of *EZ Streets*.

For the first week of unemployment, Savage marinated his brain in cheap scotch. By the time he rid himself completely of his hangover, he'd been off the force for almost two weeks. That was when he remembered Kilbey and the four million dollars. Savage had forgotten all about it because of the heat Burns started putting on him in 1983. Savage had dropped his extracurricular activities, such as dealing with Traci Miller, but IA nabbed him nonetheless. (What proved Savage's undoing was his habit of cutting corners to solve cases.)

In November 1995, Savage—one hundred percent sober—returned to the plant where Kilbey had stashed the money. The plant had been closed for five years, so breaking and entering was easier than getting a blowjob from a drunk college girl.

Savage searched the plant but couldn't find the money. The plant was too freaking huge. Kilbey could have hidden the four million anywhere.

The next day, Savage started tracking down Kilbey. It took some legwork and bribing, but after six weeks, Savage got a hold of Kilbey's e-mail address. Savage then paid a hacker to tap into Kilbey's Yahoo account. Savage practically high-fived himself when he discovered Kilbey corresponded with Marsh several times a year. Eventually, Kilbey and Marsh alluded to the *suitcase*, their keyword for the hidden money. It was all coming back to Savage.

In 1998, Kilbey sent Marsh an e-mail with the subject line: suitcase. In the body of the e-mail, Kilbey wrote: five years.

Five years? What did that mean? Savage soon found out. After a few more e-mails, he pieced together that Kilbey and his crew would meet in May of 2003 to retrieve the money. Savage wondered why they were waiting so long. Maybe they were afraid the Treasury Department knew about the money and had issued a bulletin to banks on serial numbers to look out for. If that was the reason for Kilbey's waiting, Savage had to admit, it was smart for a bunch of dipshits like Kilbey and his friends to think of (even though the Treasury Department wasn't aware of the four million).

Savage opened his eyes and pulled out a cigarette. Lighting it, he felt the Bic lighter warm his face. He dragged on the cigarette and was glad for one thing. When Kilbey did come for the money, Savage wouldn't have to worry about the unannounced arrival of associates of the dead drug dealers. He had done his Internet homework. The two syndicates connected to the shootout in May 1983 weren't a concern. Members who weren't at the industrial park that Saturday night were either long dead or had no idea of the missing four million.

Savage inhaled the last drag of his cigarette. He exhaled through his nose, like a dragon.

CHAPTER 59

4:00 A.M. on a Friday morning in May. Most Philadelphians were still in bed, relishing the last few hours of sleep before sunrise. The only people up at this ungodly hour were insomniacs, alcoholics, club crawlers, workers on the graveyard shift and, of course, Chase, Monique, Nick, Steve and Spanky.

Chase parked the Astro Van in front of the plant where the money was hidden. He cut the engine and headlights. Darkness ensued. The street's lone utility pole had a blown-out bulb (or was set to turn off extremely early) and the sun wasn't supposed to rise for at least another ninety minutes.

Nobody in the van said anything. A commercial jet passed overhead, slicing through the silence like a shout in a monastery.

"Twenty years," Chase said. "Can you believe it?"

"Ready?" Nick asked.

Chase nodded.

"Be careful," Monique said, "both of you."

"Ain't nothing but a little thing," Nick said, then turned serious. "Don't worry. I'll take care of your pooh bear."

Chase kissed Monique quickly on the lips.

"C'mon," Nick said, "let's get this party started."

Chase said to Steve, "Take care of Monique."

"Will do," Steve replied, not making eye contact.

"Let's go," Chase said to Nick.

In their black outfits, Chase and Nick scaled the plant's chainlink fence. The barbed wire at the top gave them no trouble because they both wore black Doc Martins with rubber soles thicker than boxing gloves; they simply trod on the barbed wire and leapt down to the ground. Once on the other side of the fence, they strode across the yard towards the main building. Glass and gravel crackled under their feet. Nervous energy pounded in Chase's skull.

CHAPTER 60

Pierce Price's Spyder sat in the parking lot that had once belonged to the High Street Diner. Once again, from the angle the Mitsubishi was positioned at, Price could see the plant and the Astro Van, but Kilbey and his friends couldn't see the Spyder. Besides, the night was still dark enough to act as camouflage.

Price sat in the passenger seat. Savage lazed behind the steering wheel, peering through a pair of night-vision goggles.

"What are they doing?" Price asked.

"Two of them just jumped the fence. They're inside." Savage placed the goggles on the dashboard. "Can't make 'em out no more."

"Let me see," Price said, moving for the night-vision goggles.

"No."

Price froze. "Why not?"

"Because I said so," Savage said.

Price opened his door, the interior light clicking on. Savage slapped a meaty hand on Price's wrist. The grip hurt. Price tried not to wince.

"Where do you think you're going?" Savage said.

"To—ah—uh—follow them."

"Close that door."

Price did as ordered. He stared at his hands in his lap.

Savage said, "We wait till they come out."

"Don't you want to know where they hid the money?"

"Could care less."

"So when they exit, we accost them?" Price asked.

"Yes, we *accost* them."

"You don't have to make fun."

"Shut up."

"I'm only saying—"

Savage yelled in Price's face: "I said shut the fuck up!"

Price's knees knocked together. The vibrations of Savage's yell resonated in his chest for seconds afterwards. A couple spittles, courtesy of Savage, had landed on Price's eyelids. He wiped them away, hand shaking.

Price couldn't wait to get away from this control freak. Once he got his share of the four million dollars, he was one hundred percent out of here. Back to the West Coast. *Wham, bam, I hope I never see you again, man.*

CHAPTER 61

Steve sat in the Astro Van's driver seat. He laid his left arm on top of the steering wheel and looked in the back of the van. There lounged that smelly seal. It splashed around in its tub of ice water. Steve wanted to go back and kick that seal and its leaky, rusty tub out the rear doors. Once it was out in the street, flaying around helplessly, Steve would hop out and club it to death. You could make an impressive profit from the pelt of a harp seal. Plus, last Steve heard, in the Far East, a remedy for impotence was the harp seal penis.

Steve quit thinking about the seal and surreptitiously turned his attention towards Monique. She sat in the passenger seat. God, was she gorgeous. At thirty-seven, she was as beautiful now as she was in high school. Steve couldn't help but be amazed. It was rare for a beautiful teenager to become a gorgeous thirty-something. That sure didn't happen with his wife. Her vodka problem and fondness for Devil Dogs obliterated any good looks she might have once had. *Fat fucking pig.* But that wasn't the case with Monique. No, she took care of herself, and she had a good personality, too. Her only flaw was her choice in men. Or should Steve say *man*: Chase Kilbey. Christ, what a poor choice for a husband. With each passing year, Steve hated Chase more and more. Always prancing around, thinking he was hot shit. But he wasn't, was he? He was nothing but a failed actor. *Hah!* Steve thought. *I'm a success and you're a failure. How do you like those fates, motherfucker? I'm rich and you're nothing but a pauper!*

Monique slid out of her seat, tucking one of her curls of hair behind her ear. She gave Steve a polite smile, then headed to the back of the van.

Steve formed a fist. Monique's insincere smile reminded him of the phony female executives he dealt with on an almost daily basis. They would come to meetings acting masculine but playing up their femininity with knee-length skirts and push-up bras. Steve fucked them every chance he got. Both in the boardroom and in the bedroom. *Fucking sluts got what was coming to them.*

In the back of the van, Monique petted the stupid seal. She did so while bending over, showcasing her bodacious butt. Steve licked his lips.

CHAPTER 62

Nick and Chase stood in the main building of the plant. They were in the same spot as twenty years ago, when Steve's gizmo had paged Mr. Kilbey. Both Nick and Chase wore headlamps, similar to the ones they wore in 1983.

Nick looked up. The beam of his headlamp scanned the ceiling. The light wasn't strong, but it illuminated some of the numerous holes in the building's roof, obviously the result of natural erosion. A plane flew overhead, visible through one of the holes.

Chase grabbed Nick's arm. "Did you hear that?"

"What, the plane?" Nick asked.

"No." Chase let go of his friend's arm. "Listen."

Nick listened but heard nothing except the plane fading away. "It was probably just the wind or something."

"It sounded like chains clanging together," Chase said.

"This place is pretty old. I'm sure there's some chains still strapped up somewhere."

"Yeah, you're probably right."

"I mean," Nick said, "look at this place. Half the machines are still here."

"You're right," Chase said.

"C'mon."

They strode down the corridor that led to the cave. The corridor looked as it did twenty years ago, but dirtier. Most of the paint had flaked off the walls. And most of the pipes that ran along the corners of the ceiling had broken free from their brackets; those pipes now lay on the floor. But some brackets held onto their pipes. In those cases, the pipes dipped to the floor at forty-five degree angles, looking like playground slides.

Nick and Chase reached the part of the corridor where the vat used to be. It was gone, but the ground was indented, a testament to its fifty-year presence.

Chase stopped. "Uh, what happened to the vat?"

"Damned if I know," Nick said. "My father wasn't the one who worked here. C'mon, we gotta keep moving. It'll be light out pretty soon."

They went a couple more yards, their headlamps lighting the way. They reached the cave entrance.

Chase tore off his headlamp. "Aw, you got to be kidding me!"

Nick rubbed his jaw. He couldn't believe it.

A chainlink fence filled the entrance of the cave.

Chase kicked the fence. A small tin sign on the other side flipped over. It clung to the fence via two black twisty-ties. The sign read: DO NOT ENTER. PROPERTY OF MAMMON BANK.

Chase stomped around, spitting out euphemistic expletives. He was wearing his headlamp again. The light beam raced around the walls, like a strobe light.

"Shit," Nick mouthed, studying the fence. It was strung between two hollow metal poles. The poles, about three inches in diameter, were cemented into the ground.

Nick sensed Chase standing next to him. They each leaned a forearm on the fence.

Obviously calmed down, Chase said, "They really don't want anyone going back there, do they?"

"I don't think it's that," Nick said. "I think they don't want anybody coming in here."

"What are we going to do?"

"What any freethinking human being does in the face of adversity. Improvise."

"Huh?"

Nick led the way back up the corridor. "We're in an abandoned plant that hasn't been completely cleared out, right? There's bound to be some tools lying around here somewhere."

"Right!" Chase said.

They broke into a jog, their footsteps echoing.

CHAPTER 63

Outside, down the street from the plant, Savage opened the Spyder's sunroof. A warm breeze skipped over his scalp. He yawned.

"Will you look at that?" Price said.

"Will you shut up," Savage said.

Price pointed towards the opened sunroof. "Look, a full moon!"

Frowning, Savage glanced up. A full moon peered down at Mother Earth. "You always this easily amused, Price?"

"I consistently have good luck when there's a full moon."

"Is that a fact," Savage said, picking a clump of wax from his ear.

"Yes."

At that moment, Savage decided Price deserved to die. Savage wouldn't kill him now. He'd wait until after they snatched the four million from Kilbey. Then Savage would kill Price after snuffing Kilbey and his crew. Savage would kill Price by shooting him. Start with the feet, work up to the knees and groin—maybe kick him in the gut for good measure—and if Price was still alive, shoot him in the head and heart.

Price said, "I lost my virginity under a full moon."

"Is that a fact," Savage said.

"I also made my first sale under a full moon. I have a good feeling about tonight."

Savage smirked. *Me too.*

CHAPTER 64

Chase and Nick only spent twenty minutes searching the plant for a tool to cut through the fence, and they didn't even have to leave the building. Technically, Chase found the tool, except he didn't know what it was, so he tossed it onto a nearby workbench. Nick walked by five minutes later and said, "Hey, we can use that."

The tool was a heavy-duty cable cutter. It was two feet in length, in the shape of a V, with the cutter at the bottom—its handles were made of fiberglass, and it had large rubber grips. The blades were a little dull, Nick told Chase, but they would have to do.

Carrying the cable cutter, Nick ran down the corridor to the cave. Chase followed, wondering if the cutter was hurting Nick because it banged against his leg. But that thought evaporated as they returned to the cave entrance.

Nick cut through the fence, starting at the bottom, next to one of the poles. He cut through four steel wires and was moving for a fifth one, when he stopped, dropped the cable cutter and jumped away from the fence. Chase glanced at Nick, then looked at the fence.

On the other side of the fence was a bat. Standing upright, it hooked its feet on one of the steel wires. It spread its wings and shrieked. Chase covered his ears. It was the worst sound he ever heard. Sounded like a cross between fingernails scratching a blackboard and a subway train screeching to a halt.

"What the fuck?" Nick said.

The bat's shrieking continued. Chase gawked. He could see inside the bat's pink mouth at the peak of each shriek. And when the bat wasn't shrieking, its eyes bulged, and its ears perked up, although its left ear had a little nick on the side.

"What are we going to do?" Chase shouted over the shrieking.

"Finish cutting through the fence," Nick said, standing up, "and hope that bat doesn't have rabies."

Chase gulped. "Okay."

Suddenly, Chase heard vast amounts of flapping. Soon, an army of bats clung to the other side of the fence.

"I never thought I'd say this," Chase said, "but maybe we should forget about the money."

Nick shook his head. "I think I know what's going on here. C'mere. Hold this flap up."

Reluctantly, Chase knelt down and held up the piece of fence Nick had been cutting. Chase had trouble holding it up. He was shaking like a trauma victim.

The bats swarmed for the fence flap. Nick cut another link in the fence, dropped the cable cutter, then helped Chase pull up the flap. The bats flew out of the cave through the hole in the fence. Chase's hands grew sweaty; he was grateful that Nick held the flap up, too. The bats continued their exodus, ignoring Chase and Nick. *There has to be at least a hundred of them*, Chase thought. The bats shot down the corridor, single file, in a black streak.

Chase and Nick let go of the fence flap, the entire fence undulating. Chase wiped his shaky, sweaty hands on his pants.

"How did you know they just wanted to get out, and not attack us?" Chase asked.

"Lucky guess," Nick said, picking up the cable cutter. He cut through more wires of fence before answering seriously. "This fence looks kinda new, so I guessed the bank only put it up pretty recently. The bats probably had no other way of getting out."

"You think the bank knew the bats were here when they put the fence up?"

"Probably. They may have even put it up during the day, when the bats were sleeping." Nick tossed the cable cutter aside. "I think we're ready. Hold this flap up, will ya?"

Chase did so. Nick crawled through the hole, after which he held the flap up for Chase.

"Look out!" Chase said.

A bat flew towards Nick. He froze. The bat retracted its

wings and landed on Nick's shoulder at a forty-five degree angle.

"What the..." Chase said, wondering if the bat's yellow nails were piercing Nick's skin.

Nick smiled. "How weird is that? A friendly bat."

"Hey, that's the bat that was shrieking like a banshee."

"Really? How can you tell?"

"It has a nick in its ear," Chase said.

"Ah-hah."

Chase and Nick simultaneously—wordlessly—moved for the spot where the money was hidden. Chase noticed the bat didn't leave Nick's shoulder, although it did shift as Nick moved.

"Yo," Nick said, "what the fuck?"

The hiding spot had been disturbed. The rock was pushed aside. A thick cobweb covered the hole they had hidden the money in. Chase poked a hole in the middle of the spiderless web and brought it down by creating a circle, starting in the center and moving outward. The web stuck to his hand like cotton candy. But he didn't pay too much attention to that. He was too busy staring inside the hole in the wall. The empty hole in the wall. The one without a shred of the four million they crammed in there in 1983.

Panic shot through Chase. He tried standing. Eventually making it to his feet, he was forced to reach for the granite wall to prevent a fall.

"I—I—I don't understand," Chase said, hand massaging forehead.

"Did you ever tell your brother about what we did?"

"Huh?" Chase was having trouble thinking. "What?"

"Remember you said him and you used to come down here and play when you were kids? Did you ever tell him about the money?"

"No, why would why I? I hardly see him, what with him being a priest out in Michigan and all."

Nick nodded. "C'mon, let's get back."

Chase held up the fence flap. Without urging, the bat flittered off Nick's shoulder and flew through the hole in the fence. It didn't wait for Chase and Nick. It flew down the corridor. Out of sight.

Once they were on the other side of the fence, Chase asked Nick, "Do you think the bank, or whoever put the fence up, moved the money?"

"I doubt it."

They jogged down the corridor.

"And the thing is," Nick said, "we don't have time to search the whole plant. It's almost light out. If a cop car cruises by out front, we're fucked."

"So the money's gone?"

"Looks that way."

"What do you think the bank did with the money?" Chase asked.

"Personally, I think that cock-knocker Steve took it."

"Steve?"

"Yeah," Nick said. "Think about it. He never did say where he got the money to start his company."

"Steve?"

They reached the end of the corridor, where it spilled into the main aisle. The sun was beginning to rise. A ray of celestial light squeezed through a hole in the roof.

Chase stopped when Nick grabbed his wrist.

"You hear that?" Nick said.

"Hear what?"

"Sounds like chains clanging."

"No, I don't h—"

Chase cut himself off. He heard it. It was the same sound he'd noticed when they first entered the building. He knew what it was now. *Not good.*

192

CHAPTER 65

From underneath the shadow of a workbench strutted a Doberman pinscher. Nick turned. Standing in the doorway was a German shepherd. Past the shepherd, Nick could see the Astro Van parked on High Street. He did a slow 180 and saw the Doberman standing in the aisle, acting as a hurdle to both the other exit and the corridor.

"Fuck," Nick said.

"What are we going to do?" Chase asked.

"I don't know."

The dogs were moving closer, the chains around their necks jangling.

In the distance, thunder rumbled. Chase jumped. The German shepherd barked. The Doberman joined in. The barks by themselves weren't frightening; the shepherd was low in volume and the Doberman was high-pitched. Combined, however, the barks were threatening enough to make Grizzly Adams quake in his Levi's. Nick did his best to remain calm. It wasn't easy with the barking resonating in his chest.

Out of nervous habit, Nick went to tap his right leg with his hand. He realized he was carrying the cable cutter.

"Stay close to me," Nick said.

Chase nodded.

Nick ran towards the German shepherd. Both dogs barked quicker, louder. (The Doberman remained several feet behind Nick and Steve, blocking the corridor.) Nick, still running, held the cable cutter in front of himself with the blades facing his chest. The German shepherd leapt towards Nick's throat. Nick aimed the V-shaped handles of the cable cutter for the shepherd's stomach. The handles landed on either side of the dog. Nick squeezed the handles, limiting the shepherd's malevolent movements. The shepherd flayed its legs. With help from the cable cutter, Nick held the shepherd away at arm's length. The shepherd's sharp claws didn't scratch Nick, but he did feel the dog's hot breath on his neck. He couldn't hold the shepherd up in the air much longer. Besides the strain on his arms and back, the shepherd's rapid barking was making him deaf. Nick turned and threw the shepherd but didn't let go of the cable cutter. The shepherd crashed into the oncoming Doberman. They tumbled over each other in a ball of canine confusion.

"C'mon," Nick said, "let's go!"

He and Chase sprinted out of the building, into the yard.

CHAPTER 66

In the back of the van, Monique petted Spanky. Out of the corner of her eye, she saw a black streak shooting through the entrance/exit of the plant's main building. Were they…bats?

Suddenly, Monique felt something behind her. She turned around. Steve leapt at her with the vigor of Sauron on steroids. He pinned her against the back door. Her right arm was sandwiched between her butt and the door; her left arm was free, but Steve was at an angle where pushing him away proved to be an exercise in futility. He began dry-humping her thigh in measured strokes.

"I've always wanted you," Steve panted in Monique's ear.

Monique shivered, Steve's halitosis not helping matters. Spanky, befuddled, stared at the two of them.

Steve planted his elbows on the Astro Van's windows, above Monique's shoulders. He clutched her hair and rubbed his nose on her forehead. She scrunched her face and shrank back, the edge of one of the van's two rear windows digging into her spine.

Steve stopped grinding against Monique, though his skull didn't leave the proximity of her face.

What was he doing? (Besides mopping her face with his greasy hair.)

Monique spit out a huge flake of dandruff and saw that Steve was hastening to unbuckle his pants. Since her right arm was no longer sandwiched between her butt and the door, she thought quicker than Samuel Gompers during contract negotiations.

Monique scrambled for the rear door handle.

CHAPTER 67

Chase and Nick finally finished darting across the yard. *Feels like we covered ten football fields, not 150 yards*, Chase thought.

They reached the fence. Chase started climbing. Nick didn't. He threw the cable cutter at the chasing dogs. One of the cutter's handlebars whopped the German shepherd on the side of the head. The shepherd staggered. The Doberman stopped running to visually inspect its comrade.

Chase reached the top of the fence. He stepped on the barbed wire. Nick was right behind him.

CHAPTER 68

Savage sat in the Spyder. He rubbed his two-day-old beard. The sun continued to rise, lighting up High Street like the final act of a monumental play. A small chartered plane coasted overhead.

Savage saw Kilbey and Marsh scaling the fence. He didn't see either of them carrying the money, but that didn't mean anything. One or both of them could have hidden it under their shirts or down their pants.

"It's showtime," Savage said.

Savage and Price exited the Spyder. They stalked down the street like two reservoir dogs.

CHAPTER 69

Nick was halfway up the fence when he halted. He glanced down. The German shepherd had him by the cuff of his pants.

"Motherfucker," Nick muttered.

Chase was on the other side of the fence, the side without any psycho dogs.

Nick tried yanking his cuff free of the German shepherd, but the pants were well made. They wouldn't rip.

The German shepherd stared up at Nick with the intensity of a Clive Barker villain. The shepherd's right eye was so bloodshot, Nick couldn't tell where the iris ended and the sclera began. The shepherd also had a cut from its right ear to its neckline. Nick shook his head in amazement. Throwing the cable cutter at the shepherd had done a hell of a lot of damage. Nick was glad he wasn't on the receiving end.

Meanwhile, the Doberman repeatedly jumped up in an effort to grab Nick's other leg but wasn't having much luck because the punk rocker wouldn't keep his free leg still.

"Shit," Nick said. The German shepherd yanked hard on his cuff. Nick slipped down the fence. Evidently, a knock in the head didn't sap the shepherd of much strength.

On the sidewalk, Chase was pacing—obviously brainstorming.

Nick clutched the fence, but the German shepherd's fierce tug was winning. Nick slipped a couple more inches down the fence. It didn't help matters that the shepherd's drool ran across his ankle. Even though Nick's sock absorbed most of the drool, the sensation of doggie slobber on his leg made him weak.

"Chase," Nick said, "help!"

"I don't know what to do." Chase still paced on the sidewalk.

"The stick!"

In the street lay a tree branch. Chase picked it up and stuck it through the chainlink fence. The branch poked the German shepherd on the underside. The shepherd immediately released Nick. A loud tearing sound filled the yard. Nick's cuff was now property of the shepherd. Apparently not one for mementos, the shepherd tossed the cuff aside. The Doberman dove for it.

Nick clambered up the fence. He was so happy to be away from the German shepherd that when he reached the top of the fence, he didn't bother stepping over the barbed wire. He crawled over it on his hands and knees. The barbwire pierced his palms, but he didn't care. Anything to get out of that yard.

Nick practically ran down the other side of the fence. Soon, he was standing next to Chase. Both of them looked through the fence.

In the yard, the German shepherd threw a tantrum. It crouched down, barking louder than ever, its underside grazing the ground. The Doberman barked, too, although it seemed halfhearted, as if it were only doing so to make its comrade feel better.

"Chase!"

Nick and Chase whipped around. Monique, crying, ran towards them. She threw her arms around her husband and buried her face in his neck.

"What?" Chase said. "What is it?"

Out from the back of the Astro Van hopped Steve. Pants down at his knees, he sneered and leered.

"What's going on?" Chase asked Monique.

Spanky slid out of the van. He skedaddled across the street, where Nick, Chase and Monique stood. Steve remained next to the van, pulling up his Ralph Lauren pants and buckling his Gucci belt.

A gunshot ripped through the morning air.

CHAPTER 70

Spanky was undulating across the street when he froze. He heard a gunshot. Before he could assume a defensive position, the shot tore through his body. He collapsed, his chin slamming onto the asphalt. He rolled to his side and saw that before the bullet entered his body, it bore through his left fin, creating a nickel-size hole. Blood streamed down the fin. He rolled over to make sure the bullet wasn't still inside him. No, it wasn't. He knew this for a fact because his right fin was gory and gruesome. When the bullet exited his body, it must have slit his fin like a knife. Now, his bloody right fin dangled from his body by a thread. But there was no pain. He found that hard to believe. He took stock of himself. Odd. He felt no pain whatsoever. Sure, he felt unwell, like suffering from indigestion and heartburn after eating too many exotic fish, but he wasn't experiencing any major discomfort. None yet, at least. *Maybe Spanky in shock.* That thought faded to make room for the memory of his mother being clubbed on a glacier south of Newfoundland. He wondered if when the hunter with apathetic eyes skinned his mother alive, did she feel how he felt now? Surreal.

A scream snapped Spanky out of the past.

"Spanky!"

It was his human friend, Monique. She was standing on the sidewalk next to her mate, Chase, and their fellow tribal member, Nick. Monique's hands were clenching Chase's left biceps.

"Oh my God!" Monique let go of Chase. Her hands covered her nose, mouth and most of her cheeks.

A pang of sadness filled Spanky, not for himself but for his human friend, Monique. She was so kind, so nice, so smart, so loving...such a wonderful human being. She would mourn for a long time after he was gone. He paused. *Will Spanky die?* he thought. Yes, he would. There was no doubt in his mind. Pain was settling in. It filled him from nose to tail fin. Intuitively, he knew he wasn't giving up. He was mortally wounded. Time to join his mother. But first, he had to spend one last moment at Monique's side. She wasn't moving for him.

Spanky pushed himself across the street. He used every last bit of life to reach the sidewalk. He was almost there when he ran out of gas. Rolling over on his back, he heard (but did not feel) his right fin tear from the thread it was hanging from. It made a sound similar to a harpoon stabbing a whale.

Spanky stared up at the sky. Dawn was still fighting with nighttime to give daybreak its due. The sky was navy blue. Spanky could still see the moon. It was a translucent white. He wondered if on the other side of the moon laid seal heaven. Would members of Greenpeace who'd rescued him be up there?

Monique filled Spanky's field of vision. Her head was upside-down at two o'clock.

"Oh my God, Spanky," she said, kneeling.

Spanky sensed Monique's arms wrap around him and give him a hug. He looked down and saw he was lying half in the street, half on the sidewalk. He also saw a streak of blood from here to where he was shot. His fur from the neck down was now crimson.

"Hang on, Spanky," Monique said, "we'll take you to a vet and help you get better."

Spanky's eyelids fluttered. In the plant yard, the German shepherd and Doberman pinscher whined quietly.

"Spanky!"

Monique said something else, but Spanky didn't hear words, only emotion.

Such a nice human being. You, Monique, a great human friend. Spanky love you.

Spanky stiffened and died.

CHAPTER 71

Bruno Savage, twelve-gauge sawed-off shotgun in hand, swaggered down High Street, his unwashed trench coat billowing. Pierce Price was right behind him.
    Nick addressed Savage. "Who the hell are you?"
    "What the…?" Chase said. "What are you doing here?"
    "What's up, moron?" Price said, giggling.
    "Shut up," Savage said.
    Price quit giggling.
    "The money," Savage said. "Where is it?"
    "It ain't there," Nick said.
    Savage stuck his shotgun in Nick's face. "You're lying."
    "Fuck off," Nick said. "Take your crummy Dirty Harry imitation elsewhere. Chase, who is this clown?"
    "I don't know, but this one is my boss."
    "From California?"
    "That's him," Chase said.
    Nick turned to Price. "Cally's a long way from Philly. What did you do, make a wrong turn off the Interstate?"
    Price didn't retort because Monique shrilled, "Why?" She was sitting on the curb, cradling the dead Spanky. Her cheeks were wet with tears.
    "Why?" Savage shrugged. "I hate animals. They should never leave the forests and seas they came from. You! Over here."
    "Me?" Steve said.
    "Yeah, you Atkinson. Now!"
    Steve, pants pulled up and buckled, jogged across the street from the Astro Van to join his high school buddies.
    "Chase," Monique said, "he attacked me."
    "Who," Chase asked, "the guy with the gun?"
    "No. Steve."
    Chase gawked at the computer tycoon. "Steve?"

Noir Reunion

"Fuck you, Chase!" Steve said. "Yes, I made a move on her. She needs to be fucked by a winner like me, not a loser like you. Fucking waste-oid!"

"Steve?"

"Yes, me. And you know what else? Want to know why you never made it as an actor? Because I did everything in my power to make sure none of the major players in Hollywood hired you. Fucking dick!"

"Wha—what?" Chase said.

Savage waved his shotgun around, silencing everyone. "Enough of this drama. Now where's the money?"

But before anyone could reply, Savage felt a searing pain starting in his hand and traveling up to his shoulder. He looked down at his hand, the one holding the shotgun, and gasped. He couldn't see his hand. Something black surrounded it.

"What the fuck?" Savage said quickly, panicky. He glanced up. Price, Kilbey, Flemming, Marsh and Atkinson took a collective step back.

Savage still couldn't figure out what covered his hand and caused the immense pain up to his shoulder. Then, Savage knew what he had to do. Against better judgment, he dropped the shotgun. It clacked on the street. Nobody dove for it. Instead, Price and Kilbey's crew took another step back. Maybe they were afraid the shotgun was going to accidentally fire, or maybe they were afraid they were going to catch the affliction he had. Whatever the case, Savage had no time for their extra-caution. He had himself to worry about. Inhaling deeply, he turned his hand over. He recognized the black thing covering his hand.

A bat.

The bat continued biting into the back of Savage's hand, its wings flapping like Nosferatu's cape, its green eyes peering up at the former police detective. Savage wasn't sure, but it looked like this bat (with a nick in its ear) squinted each time before biting down to reaffirm its hold. It bit down now.

Savage screamed. This time, the pain spurted from his hand all the way to his head, creating a migraine that made his ears ache and his pupils dilate.

"Motherfucker," Savage said through grinding teeth.

He flopped his arm around, hoping to shake the bat off. Not a chance. All that did was make his free arm wiggle out of his trench coat and prompt the bat to quit flapping its wings.

Savage dropped to the ground. Tears of pain filled his eyes. He blinked a couple times to clear his vision. That's when he saw it. Lying in front of him was the shotgun. His free hand dove for it, but just as he touched the checkered grip, he froze. The bat did something he never would have predicted. It launched off his hand, flying away with a little souvenir: the skin of the back of his hand.

Savage let go of the shotgun and screamed louder than a death-row convict being electrified at 12:02 A.M. He held the back of his hand up in front of his face. Blood gushed down the sleeve of his trench coat. The wound was glassy. If Savage wiggled his middle finger a certain way, he could see knuckle bone.

But Savage didn't stare at the back of his hand for too long. Gunfire was breaking out. He spun around. On the rooftop of what was once the High Street Diner stood a figure holding an assault rifle. The shooter fired again. The German shepherd and Doberman pinscher retreated from the plant yard into the building. Bullets punctured the side of the Astro Van to Savage's left. He jumped back and tripped over his trench coat. He had forgotten that when wrestling with the bat, the coat had slipped off his body, except for his forearm above where the bat had bitten him. Savage writhed free from the clutches of his trench coat, staggering in the process and grimacing when the cuff grazed the wound on his hand. A few more bullets zinged his way, one skidding over the iron manhole cover in front of him, creating sparks; that bullet skipped across the street and was swallowed up by the gutter—it pinged down into the recesses of that subterranean world. Savage, now free from his trench coat, ran for cover. He bumped into somebody who smelled of talcum powder. Pushing whomever it was aside, Savage dove behind the back of the Astro Van.

CHAPTER 72

Chase found himself part of the domino effect of Steve being pushed by the trench coat-less man. Steve didn't lose his balance and fall; however, Chase, Monique and Nick did.

Chase started to get to his feet, but froze.

More bullets sped their way from the diner rooftop. None of the semiautomatic slugs reached Chase, Monique or Nick. Their target seemed to be Steve. Chase, crouched down, was at an angle where he saw everything more clearly and vividly than he would have liked.

Six bullets riddled Steve's face. He rose his manicured hands—as if to shield himself—a little too late. The bullets had filled his face in a counterclockwise oval pattern in less than a second. He dropped to his knees, swayed for a moment, then slammed on the asphalt headfirst. Dead, his hands lay on either side of his head. None of the bullets had exited the back of his skull.

Next on the shooter's list was Pierce Price. Unlike Steve, Price was shot only once. The bullet ripped through the center of his torso, severing his spine. A vertebra popped out, landing at Monique's feet, sounding like a wooden block hitting concrete.

Price smacked down on the street, his chest kissing the manhole cover. He had hit the asphalt so hard, his skull cracked. Brain oozed out of his ear in clumps, mixing with earwax.

Chase stared down at the double murder. Bile collected in the back of his throat. Was it possible to vomit on an empty stomach?

"Chase."

He felt Monique holding his hand. They were both kneeling in front of the corpses. Chase felt a tugging on his upper arm.

"C'mon!" Nick said. He was squatting.

"What?" Chase said.

"We need to get out of here!"

CHAPTER 73

Monique let Nick drag her over to the back of the Astro Van. He dragged Chase, too.

"Fuck," Nick said.

"What?" Monique asked.

Nick didn't answer. Leaving her and Chase behind the van, he leapt into the street. Facedown, he reached for the rifle. Only the tip of his index finger touched the butt. He grunted and stretched a little farther. Hand now around the shotgun, he started to drag it to the back of the van but let go when the shooter fired again.

A bullet hit the rear passenger tire, causing the van to shake and creating a loud WHOMP. Monique jerked and screamed. She felt Chase, who, like her, was squatting behind the van, wrap an arm around her shoulders. Air hissed out of the shot tire.

Meanwhile, Nick was dashing for the back of the van. He was almost there when a bullet struck the edge of the bumper, producing a spark. Monique flinched. Upon opening her eyes, she peripherally saw Nick (who had been running bent over) drop, duck and roll. He rejoined Chase and Monique behind the van.

Monique was glad Nick had made it back alive and unscathed from his unfruitful venture. Nonetheless, she smelled something pungent. She looked to her left. There was the paunchy man who the bat had bit.

The man was still without his trench coat. He wore camouflage cargo pants and a flannel collar shirt, the latter's top three buttons undone to reveal underneath a thin coffee-stained Hanes T-shirt. He reeked of onions and garlic.

"Out of my way," the man said. Before Monique, Nick or Chase could reply, the man opened the Astro Van's back door, climbed in and slammed the door behind him.

Nick asked, "The keys aren't in the ignition, are they?"

"No," Monique said, "I have them."

Inside the van, Monique heard the man curse. A vibration followed. She assumed the man was whacking the steering wheel with his good hand.

"What are we going to do?" Chase asked.

"I don't know," Nick said. "We don't have a lot of options."

Chase stared down the street, in the opposite direction of the diner. Monique noted that even though it was light out, the street seemed to extend into an endless, dark abyss.

"Don't even think about it," Nick said to Chase. "You want to get shot in the back? You saw what a good shot that sniper is."

"He missed you. Besides, maybe he's out of ammo."

Monique said, "We may have to make a run for it. More shooters could be on the way. If they block off the street"—she motioned to the section of the street in question—"I don't know what we're going to do."

The topic was cut short by more gunshots. Glass breaking. A bullet whizzed overhead, stopped by a wooden utility pole.

"What the..." Chase said.

"They're shooting up the windshield," Nick said.

Inside the Astro Van, the man swore. The van rocked. *He's must be taking cover*, Monique thought.

"What do you think," Nick asked, "should we go in and drive away, and hope that cop isn't a total psycho?"

"It's suicide," Monique said. "If the sniper is shooting at the windshield, whoever drives won't make it out alive." Beat. "Cop?"

"Yeah," Nick said. "Cop, ex-cop, whatever the hell he is. I didn't recognize him at first but now I remember. He's the pig who pulled us over the night of the prom."

"Are you sure?" Monique asked.

"Ninety-nine-point-nine percent positive."

Chase began hyperventilating. That was when a half-dozen police cars arrived on the scene without the pomp and circumstance of flashing lights and wailing sirens, although the heat of their engines was inescapable.

Johnny Ostentatious

A plain-clothes police officer stepped out of the cruiser closest to Monique, Chase and Nick.

CHAPTER 74

Richard Avila got out of his unmarked car. In his twenty years on the Philadelphia police force, he had risen to Chief Inspector of the Detective Bureau. He still looked like a Spanish soap-opera star, but he was no longer a playboy. Last month, he and his college sweetheart had celebrated their fifteenth wedding anniversary. And next month, his three children, triplets, were graduating from grade school.

"Sir!" A flatfoot jogged up to Avila. "They got the sniper. They're bringing him around now."

"I'm pretty sure it's a she," Avila said.

"Sir?"

"Bring her around."

"Right away." The flatfoot hurried away, handcuffs on his belt jangling.

Avila turned and made a beeline towards Chase and Monique Kilbey and Nick Marsh. The Kilbeys watched him approach with frightened eyes. Nick didn't.

Avila met each one in the eye and said, "Nick Marsh, Chase Kilbey, Monique Kilbey. My name is Richard Avila. I'm with the Philadelphia Police."

Nick: "Yo."

Chase: "Hi."

Monique: "Hello."

Avila: "I'm sorry about your friend. Unfortunately, our SWAT team didn't move in fast enough to save him."

"He's not our friend," Chase said. "He was…a long time ago, but apparently hasn't been for years."

Avila nodded.

"What the hell's going on here?" Nick said.

"We've been tailing that man for some time now." Avila pointed at the Astro Van. Three cops yanked Savage out from underneath the glovebox. They kicked him into a police cruiser and slammed the door before he was all the way in. "His name is Bruno Savage," Avila said. "He used to be a cop, and not a very good one, I'm afraid."

In the cruiser, Savage pressed his forehead against the window. "Fuck you, Avila! You're still a fuckin' mommy's boy. Hey, word down the Detective Bureau is that you can't get any pussy because *you are* a pussy. Fuckin' pansy boy!"

Avila ignored the disgraced detective and spoke to Chase. "Savage has been keeping tabs on you for several years, Mr. Kilbey."

Chase went rigid, as if poked with a stun gun.

"Apparently," Avila said, "Savage knew about the money you stashed here in 1983. He enlisted the aid of your employer, Pierce Price. But unknown to either of them, someone else knew about the money, too."

Two flatfoots brought up the sniper who had killed Steve Atkinson and Pierce Price.

"Oh my God," Monique said, "Mom!"

CHAPTER 75

Chase's legs felt as if they'd been injected with blubber. Was this really Monique's mom? The one who'd divorced Mr. Flemming because he wasn't rich or important enough? The one who'd had minimum contact with Monique over the past twenty-five years? The one who'd held a series of six-figure sales jobs until she married into high society?

Yes, it was.

Chase had only seen pictures of Mrs. Flemming taken before the divorce. In those photos from the 1970s, she looked glamorous, even though she had Farrah hair; now, her hair was dyed bleached blonde. She was much shorter than Chase had imagined. And her cheeks stretched back toward her ears. Obviously, she was the recent victim of a novice plastic surgeon, or she'd undergone so many facelifts that she failed to look human, like Joan Rivers.

"Hello, Monique," Mrs. Flemming said, "you're looking well."

Mrs. Flemming wore a mink stole, a black V-neck moiré taffeta blouse, white rayon/cotton pants and black spike high heels.

"Oh, and this must be your husband. Chase is it?"

Mrs. Flemming's gaze then fell on Nick. She sneered.

Avila cleared his throat and addressed Chase, Monique and Nick. "The reason the money wasn't where you hid it is because Mrs. Dwyer"—he motioned towards Monique's mother—"obtained it in December of 2001. She learned of it through Mr. Atkinson."

"What?" Chase said. "How?"

"She and Mr. Atkinson had been having an affair for several years," Avila said.

"Omigod." Monique knelt down. Chase joined her, squatting and hugging her.

"Holy shit," Nick said. "So, Steve and Monique's mom are

married to other people, but they're fucking each other on the side. Then one night, there's some pillow talk where Steve babbles about where we hid the money."

"Correct," Avila said.

"But why?" Nick asked.

"I wish to speak to my lawyer," Mrs. Flemming said.

"Take her away," Avila told the two flatfoots.

Chase watched Monique's mother escorted away. She carried herself as if royalty on the way to a ball. Head high, swaggering gait.

"Apparently," Avila said, "Atkinson's company was on the verge of bankruptcy after the technology craze bottomed out in 2000. We believe Mrs. Dwyer gave him half of the four million dollars. It was enough to keep his business solvent. He and his accounting firm tried being 'creative' about the money during an IRS audit, but Atkinson, Inc. was already in too much trouble with tax law violations."

"Really?" Nick said.

Avila nodded. "He was claiming deductions only nonprofits are entitled to."

Chase said, "I wonder if the money he used to start his company was stolen, too."

"No," Avila said, "that was clean, good old-fashioned venture capital."

Nick stared at the Chief Inspector.

"My wife works for the IRS," Avila explained.

"Why did my mom try to kill us?" Monique asked.

Avila answered, "Mr. Atkinson recently 'traded her in for a younger model,' you might say. We believe that sparked a jealousy, which resulted in this." He motioned to the dead bodies of Price and Atkinson.

"So," Nick asked, "what happens to us?"

"You'll be arrested but released on personal recognizance bonds. You'll eventually be tried for tampering with a crime scene, and I'm sure the D.A. will want to add other miscellaneous charges—misdemeanors mostly. I'll do everything in my power to make sure none of you do time. What you all did was wrong, and you should be punished, but none of you should go to prison—there's no point in that. Besides, we live in a dysfunctional society where too much value is placed on wealth. It's understandable why you took the money. Granted, you had plenty of time to turn it in anonymously, but there are worse crimes in the world. I'm sure a judge will look at the circumstances and let you all off with community service. All right? Good. Now let's take a little ride downtown. Who feels like driving?"

Author Afterword

OK, first off, there is no such thing as a "Spenser Award Winner," as stated on the front cover. That's just a little joke to poke fun at book awards. I have yet to read a "Best Novel Of The Year" that wasn't a waste of paper and a library request. Maybe my tastes are too specific. Maybe my below average I.Q. only lets me read at too low of a reading level. Or maybe there's a lot of politics going on with those overeducated book committees.

Anyway, a little background on *Noir Reunion*: I started it in 2001 and pretty much finished it two years later, which is why the majority of it takes place in '03. When writing, I usually try not to stamp a year on the story, but I couldn't do that in this case because the roots of the plot trace back to 1983, and there are a lot of pop culture references that I wanted to keep (for the most part) factually correct. Plus, I wanted Chase, Monique, Nick and Steve to meet up twenty years later.

The reason why *Noir Reunion* took almost three years to publish is that it took a while to set up my small press, Active Bladder (I wanted to do everything legal and legit from the get-go). Also, a book of mine came out before *Noir Reunion*—*Ian Hahn: The Olfactory Empath*.

Now that Active Bladder is set up, I'll be able to devote more time to my fiction. Ideally, I'd like to release two novels of mine a year, along with one other by an author who writes suspenseful fiction in the genre of horror, mystery, romance or sci-fi.

All right, I don't know about you, but I'm getting really bored with this afterword. Thanks for letting me ramble...

Johnny Ostentatious
Philadelphia, PA
July 11, 2005